M000117303

cover photo 1249 S. Garrison
Carthage MO
circa 1948

1

Small Town Stories

Allen Dean

Copyright 2019

Index

5. Preface

8. LouElla and The Plumber

18. The War

29. The Paper Boy

38. Compound Interest

44. Daddy's Car

48. Monty and the Lathe

59. Stinky's Day

165. The Awakening

199. Club Charity

Preface

Mrs. Courtney didn't like people, at least, not in person. She did like people around though, because she was afraid to live alone. So she lived in town, fought with her neighbors, and called the police on a regular basis on Thanksgiving, Christmas, VE day and July 25th.

DeWalt Whitman was the policeman assigned to checking out Mrs. Courtney's complaints, even when he was not on duty. He had over the years on the force grown into this roll as he watched new young officers coming into the force, and knew they wouldn't understand Mrs. Courtney. Christmas and Thanksgiving were a chore to DeWalt anyway. He preferred quiet, to celebration. Maybe the preference was a holdover from his mother, who was a schoolteacher and librarian before DeWalt was born. His father Ronald had died when DeWalt was only one, and holidays had never been much to celebrate. His grandfather on his Father's side had been the only man DeWalt had around much when he was *young. Dean Whitman had not been a good influence and DeWalt's mother had not encouraged the acquaintance. DeWalt's name was a curiosity in itself. His mother's father was named Walter. His father's father was Dean, DeWalts' mother, Rose, being a librarian, naturally had a literary tendency, and being not quite sound of mind when she found she had a new baby boy, named him for both grandfathers and her favorite early American poet. Thus, DeWalt Whitman. Besides that, her husband was a carpenter and had just purchased a new DeWalt table saw. DeWalt's childhood had been trying.*

Mrs. Courtney was careful about her police calls, never making them for the same complaint two times in a row. In 1954 it was a dog digging in her back yard which growled at her and looked like it had foam on it's mouth. That was at 2:30 in the afternoon. In 1957, VE day, it was hoboes in the alley in an old truck. That was at 9:30 AM, and the Randallls were making their trash pickup rounds. In 1958 Mrs. Courtney called the police dispatcher on Christmas eve, claiming that she had a prowler. She knew that DeWalt would be busy with company on Christmas day and so had modified her routine to accommodate him. She learned later, that he sometimes wished he could get away from that noisy bunch at his house, and she never changed her schedule again.

A whole generation of grocers had learned to fear Mrs. Courtney. Tough grocery store owners and managers would blanch and hide in their low walled booths or duck into the walk-in freezers when she came in. Ground beef was one of the major bones of contention. It was always too fat, or too lean, or smelled old or looked under the weight marked on the package. She bought half a beef from Art Walters down at the Ice House in '54. She made him unwrap every piece of meat and weigh it for her as she kept tally and then watched over him as he carefully wrapped each lump of meat according to her instructions and place them in her little section of the locker, careful not to stack ground meat beneath other things. It didn't matter that it all was frozen hard as hooves. She insisted that ground beef couldn't go underneath the tongue or the steaks, it would be mashed flat.

Cheese was one of her particular peeves. She loved cheese, but it had to be right. She often bought packaged cheese, ate part of it, and then returned it saying that it was not what it was labeled. Colby tasted like mild cheddar. Mild cheddar was sharpe. American cheese tasted like Colby. Sometimes Swiss was mozzarella. Sometimes, mozzarella was Swiss. She got confused once and insisted that she had purchased swiss and it had turned to cheddar in her refrigerator. Mr. Wright proprietor of Winston's grocery, had suggested that maybe it was her refrigerator, as a means to get her off his back. Mac Jones, down at the hardware where her refrigerator had come from, never forgave Albert Wright, and the hardware store stopped handling appliances after that.

Mrs. Courtney had others on her regular list besides the police. One of her other "regulars" was George "Grunt" Andress. He was "Andress Plumbing". If you had a plugged drain or an overflowing septic tank you called "Grunt's". George finally had it listed in the phone book under both Andress Plumbing and "Grunts" because so many people got on to him about having an unlisted phone number. All agreed it was easier to remember "Grunt's" than "Andress Plumbing" when your toilet was plugged up. Grunt got a call the first time the temperature got down near freezing each winter. Mrs. Courtney was sure her water was flowing slowly and would be frozen soon. So Grunt would drop whatever he was doing and climb in his Ford truck and go. He usually parked in front of the *hospital and walked across the street to Mrs. Courtney's. She would meet him on the walk, and scold him for parking where visitors to the hospital were supposed to park.*

Grunt would always start back toward his truck to move it but Mrs. Courtney would snap "You just get right back here George Andress. I don't intend to pay you for the time you spend moving your truck."

That was just as well. Grunt never sent her a bill anyway after the first time. He sent her his regular house call bill in 1955 after Max Arnold of Arnold Plumbing died and Grunt made his first call on Mrs. Courtney. It was that first visit that set the pattern for all the years after.

LouElla and The Plumber

It was Halloween of 1955 and Monday. Grunt had just been out on his own for a few years. He had worked for Max Arnold for nearly ten years, and when Max decided to just service his old established customers and slowly move into retirement, George had gone out on his own, with Max's endorsement. Now Max had died and naturally George was picking up the "old timers" from Arnold Plumbing.

George didn't have an office girl, but he did have an answering service in the form of Ron Yates. Yates had a barbershop in the front part of the Andress Plumbing building. George had an extension phone installed inside a cabinet in the barbershop for his calls. Customers having their hair cut would be surprised when the phone would ring inside the cabinet, and Yates would open the cabinet, pick up the phone and answer "Andress Plumbing." He would then proceed to ask a few questions, carefully noting the name and the time and the complaint for when George checked in. In return for this service, Yates never payed a plumber for anything. That Halloween morning Ron Yates had gotten a call from LouElla Courtney.

"Andress Plumbing." He answered after turning off his clippers he was using to sculpt Harold Lasiter's flattop. "How may I help you?"

A voice from the phone said, "You don't sound like George Andress to me. Who is this?"

"It's Ron Yates Ma'am" He started to continue to explain, but there was a loud click as the phone was hung up on the other end.

Ron picked up his clippers, noting the white flakes stuck to them and started them back up to finish Harold's cut, thinking he would have to clean the clippers after Harold left. He had already dismissed the phone call and was concentrating on his work when the phone in the cabinet rang again. "Address Plumbing" he answered again.

"I know your voice Ronald Yates. Now you quit answering the plumber's phone." The voice was loud enough that Harold heard and recognized LouElla's voice.

"Now madam" Ron began but was cut off immediately.

"Don't you madam me Ronald Yates! You just get off that party line and let George Andress answer his telephone." and again he heard the loud bang and the line was dead.

Ron stared at the phone hand-piece a few seconds, then put it back on the phone and banged the cabinet door shut.

"I'm sorry Harold, now where was I?" Ron picked up the clippers and inspected his job thus far and began clipping off the last of the back, evening the hair up to match Harold's collar.

He was just finishing brushing off the back of Harold's shirt when the phone rang again. Ron whipped the apron off Harold and released the chair so it dropped down to it's lowest setting before opening the cabinet and staring at the phone. He fully expected the phone to stop ringing, but it went on and on, and he and Harold looked at each other and burst out laughing.

"Let me" Harold said, and reached down into the cabinet and picked up the hand-piece and held it quietly.

"Ron Yates that better not be you again!" LouElla shrieked after a few seconds of silence.

"Miss LouElla, this is Harold. How nice to hear your voice." Harold used his most ingratiating, oily, voice that he usually reserved for the partners at the law firm where he was the youngest junior partner at the tender age of twenty-seven. " I am answering the phone for Mr. Andress today Miss LouElla. How may I help you."

"Well how nice Harold. I would recognize your voice anywhere, after all you are my favorite bass in the church choir." She of course didn't mention he was currently the only bass in the choir. "I hope you are still employed by Watson, Wilson and Smith. You know they have been my attorneys for many years. You weren't fired were you

Harold?" LouElla sounded genuinely concerned, but Harold wasn't fooled.

"Oh no Ma'am." he answered. "I am still on quite good terms with the Misters Watson, Wilson and Smith." Harold could almost feel the disappointment coming over the phone line. That was one bit of gossip that LouElla wouldn't have. "I am still hoping to make it Watson, Wilson, Smith and Lasiter some day. Now, what message would you like me to convey to Mr. Andress?"

"Well thank you Harold. Here is my problem."

When she said that, Harold immediately thought, "Just one?" but he did not say it out loud.

LouElla continued. "I listened to the radio this morning and George, You know George on the radio? Well, George on the radio said it was going to freeze before midnight. Now I know George isn't always perfect on the weather, heaven knows he missed it last Fourth of July when it rained all day, but anyway he, George on the radio that is, said it was going to freeze and Max Arnold knew just how to take care of my pipes so I didn't have any nasty leaks or frozen faucets and since poor Max is gone now, God rest his soul," she took a breath here which made it sound as if it were doubtful that God would rest Max's soul at all, "So I am naturally calling George Andress, though he has never been to my house and I am sure it will be a mystery to him what Dear Max did for me each fall."

As the conversation proceeded, Ron Yates had carefully put away the tools of his trade, dropping them in the antiseptic cleaners and tossing the apron in the dirty clothes hamper. He had just finished sweeping up the clippings and depositing them into the trash can with the foot operated lid, when Harold completed the conversation, hung up the phone and put it back inside the cabinet where it belonged.

Harold picked up the pencil and pad that Ron kept the notes for Andress Plumbing in and carefully noted the time, 8:40 AM and the customer, LouElla Courtney, her address, he had forgotten to get, her phone number, fleetwood8-7073 and then made a few notes outlining her wishes for George to take care of.

"I better run Ron." Harold said as he closed the spiral notebook and put the pencil in it's place in the spine, Harold took his long wool overcoat off the rack and pulled it on. "The bosses will be thinking I am lollygaggin'." With that, he handed Ron two dollars, "Keep the change." He said and left, turning up the hill back toward the square and pulling his scarf tight around his neck as he walked.

Ron sat down in his barber chair and looked out the window as a few leaves flashed past the windows. He spun his chair around to the counter and picked up the notebook to see what Harold had put down as Mrs. Courtney's complaint. He laughed as he read, "LouElla needs her pipes thawed." Some how this struck Ron as funny and he chuckled as he repeated to himself, "Her pipes thawed indeed."

When George checked in to the barber shop at noon, Ron gave him a quick rundown of the calls he had gotten. There were four, other than Mrs. Courtney, and Yates made the most of the line Harold had written about "thawing LouElla Courtney's pipes."

George was a God fearing man and even more, an Alice fearing man, Alice being his wife, and that sort of joke made him squirm.

By the time he had checked on the other jobs and completed two of them, it was nearly five o'clock and the sun was dropping down over the western hills of town. He pulled in her driveway noting as he did so that it was just about the right width for a buggy but was inadequate for his big Ford truck with the utility bed on it. The truck's left front wheel dropped off the edge of the two concrete strips that made up the drive as he pulled in, but he never noticed at all.

He opened the front door to the utility bed and retrieved his big flashlight that ran on a lantern battery. He already had on his work overalls and a heavy coat, so he pulled a filthy cap out of his coat pocket and stuck it on his head as he walked up the drive.

"It's about time you got here George Andress."

George hadn't seen anyone, but following the sound he saw LouElla glaring through the curtains of her front window which she had cranked opened in order to speak to him. "Don't you walk on my porch with those dirty boots. You just go through the gate and come around back." and with that, LouElla cranked the window shut and he heard her throw the two locks on it.

George guessed that the gate was between the house and the garage and went that way. Just as he opened the gate, the back porch light flashed on and he heard the chain being removed from the door as he came around the house.

"The opening to the crawl space is right over here." LouElla stepped out on the back stoop and pointed around the house toward the back. "I want you to make sure, just like Mr. Arnold did, that all my pipes are ready for winter and my crawl space is nice and snug."

George wasn't sure what she meant, but he was agreeable. After all it was twenty eight dollars in his pocket to show up and twelve an hour for his labor. He lifted the big four foot square cap off the crawl space opening and dropped down into it. He folded himself up and began to crawl, but when he discovered the floor of the crawl space was covered with chat from the mining piles, he stopped and pulled his cotton work gloves from his back pocket and pulled them on. The knees on his work dungarees were double thickness but he could still feel the chat digging in. He reminded himself to keep his toes up out of the chat. His Knapp work shoes were only a few weeks old. As he pulled his gloves on, he heard the big old floor furnace near the center of the house light and he took a quick look at the vent pipe just to make sure it was safe. It looked good, and he was sure that enough heat escaped from the furnace to keep the crawl space warm on even the coldest of nights. Even with the light fading outside, he could see that the vents to the crawl space were open, so he made the trip around the perimeter walls and closed them all, finding a rectangular piece of lumber sitting along side each one, on the foundation walls, The boards fit snug, and there were two little blocks on each end that turned and held them in place. He looked at the plumbing as he moved along and saw that every pipe in the house had been wrapped in what appeared to be rags of some sort. It looked like a pretty good job to George, and after a few more minutes making sure there were no other points that cold air would infiltrate under the house, George climbed out. He maneuvered the big wooden cap back in place over the hole and stood up stretching his back. It had been a long day. He rapped on the back door and LouElla yanked it open with the first little tap.

"Are you done already?" She asked accusingly. "Are you sure my pipes aren't freezing?"

"Yes'm." He answered and then thought better and said, "No Ma'am."

"Well?" LouElla demanded. "Which is it?"

"Uh" George really wasn't equipped for this sort of conversation. "Your pipes ain't freezin' and they probably ain't gonna."

"Well I guess I will believe you, even though it took Max, that's to say Mr Arnold much longer to do the job." LouElla looked at him doubtfully. "Are you sure you checked my pipes properly?"

George wished she would stop saying that thing about checking her pipes. It made him uncomfortable because of the jokes Yates had made at lunchtime. "Well, goodnight Mrs. Courtney." he said in answer, and tapped the bill of his hat and went back to his truck and home to Mrs. Andress.

It was two weeks later when LouElla arrived at his place of business, just off the square, in back of Yates Barber Shop. She apparently was furious with George.

"George Andress", LouElla shouted, "George Andress you have tried my patience. I have here the newspaper from November second, and it says the temperature never dipped below 33 degrees on October 31 so you could not possibly have thawed out my pipes like this bill says! I won't pay it George Andress. Your Grandma would be ashamed of you!" She had charged through Yate's Barber shop and into Georges workshop before Yates could even put down his clippers.

George wasn't sure what his grandma had to do with it. Besides, one Grandma had been dead since before he was born and the other lived in Denmark and had all her life. He didn't figure either one really knew him at all, least of all the one in Denmark.

"If you try to collect this, I will call my Watson, Wilson and Smith and have them file a complaint against you with the Better Business Bureau and the prosecuting attorney's office." At this point she tore the yellow copy of the bill into shreds and stood and glared at George.

He was still standing at his work bench with one hand inside a large cast iron sewer trap when she tossed the pieces of paper in the air and pushed her way back past Ron Yates who was standing in the door with his mouth hanging open. "Close your mouth Ron Yates." she said as she went past, "You look like you are catching flies." And she skittered across the tile barbershop floor, past Leopold Randall in the barber chair, and the bell rang angrily as she went out.

George never sent another bill. He didn't need that kind of trouble.

After that first year, every once in a while Yates up in the Barber shop would try to be funny and ask in front of his customers "Hey Grunt! You been thawin' out ol' Miz Courtney's pipes lately?" He particularly liked to ask that on days when, as Yates would say "it's so hot you could fry an egg on a bald man's head". Yates liked that saying figuring that was all a bald head was good for.

George always just grinned and said "Least I got one regular customer. That's more'n you got Yates. One haircut from you is enough for a lifetime." When Grunt would say that he would yank off his dirty hat, showing hair that stuck out every which direction, rub his hand over his head changing not one hair, and then slap his hat back on. "Just look what you done to me!" Customers squirmed some when they saw this display, but none ever got up the nerve to leave. George and Yates fished together most every weekend excepting holidays or when it was near freezing or below.

Oddly, Mrs. Courtney still called every fall, near or on, Halloween and George would go and follow the same routine. He often wondered over the years who took those little boards off the crawl space vents in the spring. After the second year, he always got a cup of coffee on these calls to Mrs. Courtney's but never anything more. At first he figured he got his payment by mimicking Mrs. Courtney in the coffee shop. She always provided good material to work with. But after a few years, he even stopped doing that.

Mrs. Courtney had the mailman as a very involuntary regular visitor. When a meeting over routes was held with the carriers, there was very nearly a fist fight over boundaries being set when it was discovered that Mrs. Courtney's street was being changed. The man being given the block with her house on it claimed he was being discriminated against.

Mrs. Courtney believed in promptness and reliability. She expected to be able to set her watch by the mailman. Her time was 9:48 am and if the mailman varied at all he could expect a reprimand. When Ed Foley was running her route he ran early one morning so he could attend his kids PTA program that evening. For nearly a week afterward Mrs. Courtney called the Post Office to complain that he was late when he came at the regular 9:48 instead of at 9:33 like the one early day. Finally Ed changed his route so that he came to Mrs. Courtney's house before he went in to deliver the hospital mail and again all was tranquility. Unless of course he delivered a sale flyer when the sale had already ended.

The War

When the war started nobody noticed. It wasn't like WWII when Japan bombed Pearl Harbor and everyone knew it was war! Not that there hadn't been indications that there could be war with Japan and Germany but that the bombing of Hawaii made a nice solid comfortable point to say' "This is the beginning!" This war on the other hand, crept up with small, almost insignificant, steps. The same day Ed Foley delivered the mail thirty minutes late to Mrs. Courtney, Art Walters was late to work at The Ice House after spending the morning at the dentist. Art had never been to a dentist in his life and did not enjoy the new experience. Ed was late because of the cursed Sears Catalog. The week for the big catalog had come. Ed waved to Art as Art went by in his 49 Ford truck. Art looked the other way. He had nothing but teeth and the crick in his neck on his mind. He never even saw Ed. Ed scowled and went on back to his mail storage box for the next load. The next week Ed stopped in at the Ice house to pick up some steaks for the wife. As near as he could tell after rummaging around in the locker there were no steaks there. Ed had the only key. Art couldn't have gotten in there. But there were supposed to be steaks there. When he got home he smelled steak frying. His wife had picked them up. But all the way home he had been wondering how Art could get in his locker and take the food right out of his mouth. Art mailed out a birthday card to his mother from the Ice House mailbox. Ed was assigned to another route that day and the replacement never picked up the outgoing mail. Art saw his mother (who lived eight blocks from the icehouse) the next day, on her birthday, and she hadn't gotten her card. The following day Art complained to Ed who proceeded to explain that he hadn't done the route the day the card had not been picked up. Art understood, but for two days he had been thinking Art had just not bothered to pick up his mail.

Both men knew that the other had not really done anything wrong to the other, but those days of ill feeling were a part of them. The mind knew, but the emotions were in place and could not be dislodged.

Ill will needn't be fostered by fact. Art and Ed were beginning to feel an animosity that was generally without basis. Just a twinge when Ed saw Art. Just a quick turn of the stomach when Art saw Ed.

Art went to the Independent Methodist church north of town as did Ed. Ed was a regular and Art was an Easter, Christmas member. Art got up and just felt like going to church on this particular Sunday. It was not hunting season for anything but varmints. He figured it was too cool and cloudy to fish. There was never anything on TV on Sunday morning but preachers so he might as well go and see a live one. Besides it would surprise his wife, which was something Art could rarely manage. Missy Walters went every Sunday regular as clockwork. Little Arthur went too, but was torn between what he thought was right and what his father (lower case f) wanted him to be, which was a big tough outdoorsman. Part of the reason they attended the independent Methodist Church and not the big church in town was the fact that some of the men that attended that church hunted and fished on occasion. So Art, Missy and Arthur set off on Sunday together. Ed and Gina took separate vehicles. Dean, Ed's oldest, went with Gina. Randy, Ed's younger boy, went with him in the pickup truck. . At the time Randy was nine and was experimenting with social interaction by making faces at cars when they met them or when they pulled up to intersections. Ed was unaware of Randy's pastime being consumed with singing with the radio playing Old Country Church. Ed pulled up to the four way stop at Macon and Main and saw coming from his left another car which pulled up just after he did. He waved the other car, which was making a right turn, on, and then went on with his singing while rummaging about in his paperwork searching for the Sunday school opening exercise notes. When he looked up, the car was still sitting there and the driver was turned away from Ed, talking to a woman passenger. Ed went back to sorting papers and looking up the opening scripture and marking it with an old church bulletin left over from some past week. When he looked up again, the car was still there, so he stuck his pickup in low and lurched forward just in time to see the other driver do the same. Ed slammed on the brakes, so did the car and then they both stared at each other. Ed smiled big and waved the car on while thinking words not appropriate to use in front of Randy. Art was volubly cursing this idiot that had come to the intersection before him, and then wouldn't go first. Art figured that if he went, when it wasn't his turn, that the other driver would charge out and run into him and claim it was Art's fault. Well Art figured he was no fool, and he wouldn't go till it was his turn. But the idiot just kept messing with something and it looked like he was shouting. At least his mouth was going, and Art figured he was looking down and yelling something because he knew Art could read lips. Finally Art being exasperated, charged forward and then slammed on the brakes just in time to avoid hitting Ed Foley in his truck door. Ed waved at Art then he pulled out and turned left. Art followed along. Art remembered, about this time, that he didn't really want to sit through Sunday school. Missy was teaching a class, and little Arthur had his own class to go to, so he would be alone. He turned into the News Stand at Walnut and Garrison to get a Joplin Globe to read while Sunday school was going on. Ed recalled, just as Art turned left in front of him, that the Sunday school class had been out of coffee and he was supposed to make it that morning.

He pulled in on the opposite side of the store and went in. Art read the headlines before leisurely driving on toward the church. Ed, having purchased his can of Folgers, followed close behind. When they pulled up to the church it had begun to rain steadily and Art pulled up near the door of the church only to see an empty parking spot right by the door. Art pulled in and parked. Ed followed Art into the gravel lot expecting to pull into his reserved spot when Art Walters pulled in there and let out his family. Ed and Randy waited patiently for Art to see the reserved sign for the Sunday School Superintendent and move. The Superintendent was a jack of all trades job and often included the picking up and delivering to church young children or perhaps old folks that for various reasons no longer drove themselves. Gina was doing that duty today but Ed was still going to park in his reserved place. Art Walters turned off his headlights and unfolded a newspaper and began to read. Ed put his pickup in reverse and slammed backwards out of the lot and across to the next row of cars looking for a parking spot. The only parking spot was out near the road where, when he stepped out of the truck, he was ankle deep in a puddle. He stood in the water, picked up Randy, and carried him across the wettest place, then sat him down, held his hand, and they splashed their way to the door. They ran past Art who was placidly reading the Sunday Globe. They never noticed the "Reserved" sign from Ed's parking place, sitting, newly painted, in the foyer of the church, waiting to be put back on it's post out in the parking lot.

When the bell rang for the end of Sunday School, Art had finished the sports section, and the want adds for cars, so he carefully folded his paper, and went into the church and picked a pew. Little Arthur came in and sat next to him in a few minutes, and then Missy came and joined them. Art was listening to Alice Knight play the piano preparatory to the service and mentally making notes of the various things she was doing wrong. Art was no musician but he knew bad piano playing when he heard it. He could tell the piano was out of tune as well. Art leaned over and whispered in little Arthur's ear, "That lady playing must have had a spastic metronome when she learned to play."

"What's a spazz tick metro loom?" Arthur asked loudly.

"Shhhhh" Art shushed him, but not soon enough.

Ed Foley came in and went to his accustomed seat and found the pew already occupied by Art Walters and his family so he slid into the one directly behind his accustomed place. Little Randy and Gina came along in a few minutes and slid in with Ed. Deanna Foley sat with the teenagers a little further up and on the other side of the building. Ed's family all dutifully picked up a hymnal at the start of the song service and began to sing lustily. Art sat and looked at the backs of the people in front of him. Missy and little Arthur sang quietly. Art listened through the first two stanza's of "How Firm a Foundation" then pulled out a book and thumbed through looking at songs. On the second song he amused himself by counting the E's in "When the Roll is called Up Yonder". Then actually joined in and sang a little with "In The Garden" for the prayer song. Newton French gave the prayer and read it out of a little notebook he had. Ed felt it was a pretty poor thing to have to write down a prayer. (Actually Newton had copied the prayer from another published book violating the copyright law.) Art listened with half an ear to the announcements as he read the bulletin and found they were the same announcements he heard every Easter and Christmas. That old Farmer woman was always sick. Why didn't she just call it all off and die. He was still enjoying this thought when the announcement was made that Deana Foley and Jennifer Watts would provide the special music. Alice Knight was to accompany them. Jennifer and Mrs. Knight had written the music and Deana had written the words. Deanna had broken up with a boyfriend two weeks earlier and in a fit of melancholia had written a poem lamenting the fact that she wasn't Catholic, and therefore could not be a nun and be celibate. She had since found Jeff Hotch interesting and so had changed the words to be a religious song.

23

Waste not, want not. The girls stood up front and Mrs. Knight began to play. Then the girls each picked up a microphone and began to sing. First Deanna then Jennifer trading back and forth on each line. With each switch, Art's ears hurt a little more, and the pew became a little more unbearable. The girls sang what they considered to be harmony on the chorus but was really just singing close proximity to an octave apart. Jenifer had an alto voice and was painfully singing the high octave. Deanna had a thin soprano voice and was singing the low octave a-la Marlena Dietrich. Art snuck one finger up like he was scratching his head and stuffed his little finger in the ear nearest the loudspeaker mounted on the wall above where he sat. He never worked up the nerve to stick a finger in the other ear but he was about ready by the fourteenth and final verse. Art leaned over to little Arthur as the song ended and whispered something and little Arthur looked tickled then said loudly to his mother right next to him, "Sounds like cats fightin' don't it?"

Gina shushed him and he retorted, "Pa says!"

"Shush" from Gina.

Ed Foley heard it all. Ed's wife Missy heard it too. There were no good Methodist thoughts on that pew for the remainder of the service. Most of the other folks in church agreed with little Arthur, but hid the fact from Ed, which was just as well.

On Monday nights the YMCA had basketball for grade school age boys. The young boys, ages six through nine, played at 6:00 pm and the older boys, aged played at 7:30. The coaches would pick teams trying to be fair but both wanting to win. The first choice was always by coin toss. Jim Locks and Sammy Baker were the coaches for this season. Jim won the toss and picked Mickey

Andress. He was big for his age, fast, and smart. He was always the first pick. Second pick was always one of the Wofford boys. It didn't matter much which of the three. They all played well. After that it was pick and chose over the leavings. Sammy leaned toward picking his friends kids next. Jim tried to figure out which kid would foul up the least that particular day. Jim liked to win. It was inevitable there always had to be two boys that were chosen last. It was always Arthur Walters and Randy Foley. They were both pitiful ball players and their dads were neither one friends with the coaches. On this particular Monday, Art decided to stay at the Y and play pool while little Arthur played basketball.

Ed dropped off Randy at the YMCA, then went to the Drake Hotel for a haircut at the hotel barber shop. It was the only place he could get a haircut, working six days a week delivering mail. He rarely finished his route early enough to catch the regular barbers in town.

Art had been to the Triple L Tavern the night before. So had Dave Box. Dave Box was now in the Drake Barber Shop, recounting a story Art had told. The story was about girls that sang in church, replete with sound effects and body motions. Ed was sitting in the tall chair, letting old Grandpa Wofford shine his shoes. He was reading a Life magazine when the story started but soon picked up the thread. Art had been in rare form telling the story, and Dave Box did it justice, plus added a few lewd and suggestive items of his own.

When Ed got up in the chair and Lew started to cut his hair Ed snapped "Just cut it like you always do."

Lew Smith had been cutting hair a long time, and knew better than try to visit with this customer.

Art played pool for a few games, then tried a little ping pong, but the net kept falling down, and one leg was wobbly on the table, so that was given up. Art went in to watch the basketball teams play. He climbed up to the mid level to get a good view of the game. The first game had ended with Jim's team winning by the skunk rule in the second quarter so a new game was started with all the second string players or scrubs as Jim called them. While the new game got organized, Art went out to the restroom.

The ten best players sat on the sidelines and harassed the ones on the floor. Randy and Arthur were both on the floor on the same team. Earlier, while choosing teams, when they got down to the last choice, Coach Jim gave Arthur to Coach Sammy, as an extra. It was not a kindness. Arthur was shouting to Randy to throw him the ball. Randy often hogged the ball. Arthur got the ball a couple of trips up and down the floor later, booted the ball while dribbling and threw up a wild shot that missed the backboard and bounced off the balcony wall. Ed arrived to watch, just as, after several tries, one of Arthur's shots flew up into the balcony. Some of the older boys were lounging around up there and threw the ball back down. It bounced about midway between little Arthur and Randy. Both ran for it and collided as they both leaned over to grab it. Randy went down right where he was. Arthur stumbled a few steps then sat down with a thump.

The wail that little Arthur let out electrified big Art to action, as the entire gym was suddenly silent but for the sobbing and wailing.

Randy on the other hand rolled over on his back and just lay there stunned. Ed shot out of the entry between the bleachers out onto the floor just as Art bounded off the second bleacher. They met right at the five second line and went down in a tangle of arms and legs. Neither had seen the other.

"God bless it all!" Arthur shouted as he shoved Ed off his legs.

"Shove it, you ass!" Ed rejoined as he scrambled up, all reason lost in the confusion, both hands squeezed into tight fists.

"What the he, uh heck." Arthur restrained himself as he was confronted with two little boys standing in front of him holding hands.

"Are you OK Daddy?" Little Arthur said as he reached out and touched his father's hand with his. "Randy has a bump Daddy. Do you have a bump?"

All this time Ed had been sitting on the floor, looking at Randy's bump and little Arthur holding his hand. He rolled over on his knees and stood.

Randy sniffed loudly, and the spell was broken as the ref tossed the ball inbounds and the game was on again, replacement players in place. Art and Ed scooted their boys off of the court and walked to the bench to pick up their jackets and change to their street shoes.

Little Arthur stood and watched as Ed got down on his knees to change Randy's shoes. "Can we get Randy an ice-cream Mr.Foley? I sometimes need an ice-cream when I have a bump."

Ed looked uncomfortably at Art, and then at little Arthur, and Randy. "We can if it's my treat."

For a few years the newspaper boy was a regular at Mrs. Courtney's house, but then the paper went up to seven cents a day from the previous six cents per day, and of course Mrs. Courtney refused to pay the extra. She was struck from the list and she started her lifelong habit of walking into the newspaper office and picking up a day old paper, which was free. The only thing she really liked about the paper anyway was her old school-mate LeeRoy McGrain's historical articles. So for years, she lived a day behind everyone else. Nobody minded, much.

The Paper Boy

Anthony "Tony" Norris took his paper throwing duties very seriously. On the day of his interview to begin his career as a Carthage Press carrier, he had left school at 3:45 PM and ridden his bicycle straight to the "Press" offices downtown. He had entered the front doors only to be directed by the receptionist at the big desk, to go back out the doors, around the building, up on the loading ramp, go in the walk-in door, and ask for Mr. Parkland.

When Tony entered the battered door, he was greeted by an incredible din emanating from the basement, half a dozen boys tying up bundles of papers on a big wooden bench, and another half dozen slovenly looking adults watching over them. All of them had dirty hands. Tony was shocked. He had been schooled in cleanliness by a mother that believed "Cleanliness is next to Godliness" even if that didn't specifically appear in the Bible.

"Why were these people so grubby looking?" He wondered. Several had on filthy aprons that increased the illusion that they were completely covered by black dirt.

"Uh," Tony started, "Uh. Uh. I need to see, uh....Mr. Uh.....uh... Parkland."

"What?" One of the adults took a cigarette out of his mouth and shouted at Tony.

"Mr. Parkland!" Tony shouted, just as most of the noise coming up the ramp from the basement stopped. Most of the people in the room, surprised by the shout in the relative silence, turned and stared at Tony.

"Geez...." One of the boys said, then turned back to his duties tying the bundles and carrying them to the big overhead door that was still closed against the cool outside.

"What?" came a shout from a doorway across the loading dock on the far side of the room. "Who's shouting at me out there?"

Tony just stood there, mortified.

"Well, what do you want him for." one of the adults that may have had slightly less black hands than the others, stepped forward and asked, motioning toward the far wall leaving a trail of smoke from the cigarette in his hand.

Just then, Tony just noticed there was a window that looked in on an office.

"I, uh, I, uh," Tony struggled, "Uh... I want a job."

"Well go on then." the man pointed the way with the other hand, then started carrying newly tied bundles of papers toward the door.

"Tony made his way around the stacks, flinching away from the other boys and approached the door to the office. The cigarette smoke was practically rolling out the door and Tony's eyes watered as he entered the tiny room. He could barely see the man sitting in the semi-dark behind a huge desk piled with papers. Much of the pile seemed to consist of large metal rings with cards hanging on them. Tony remembered seeing the guy collecting for the paper at his house carrying one of them.

"Do you know what happened this month?" A coarse low voice said from behind the desk.

"Uh…." Tony had no idea how to answer the question.

"Them Ruskies is settin' off nucular bombs way up in the sky and poisoning their own people. Probably killin' the pilots flyin' them bombs too. Them Limeys set off a nucular bomb too. You should know this stuff!"

Tony had no idea how to respond so he just stood and tried to breath as little as possible while he wiped his nose that had begun to run as a result of his eyes burning and tearing from the cigarette smoke.

"Some people made a play in New York about an old book called Pygmalion and called it "My Fair Lady". It's got nothin' to do with pigs, and you should know that if you read the Carthage Press." Mr Parkland waved his hands around excitedly as he expounded on this, glaring from behind the desk at Tony. "Did you know Bill Skowron hit a baseball clean out of Fenway Park and those bum pitchers the Cubs got walked nine batters in just one inning?"

"I just want to be a paper boy." Tony said meekly.

"Well, no-body here is "just a paper boy" let me tell you." Mr. Parkland stood and leaned on his desk with both hands, showing clearly why his side of the desk was covered with cigarette burns. "You will be the harbinger of news, both good and bad. You will be the calendar and the announcer of the events of a lifetime. You will carry the glory of birth, the sadness of illness and the tragedy of death."

Tony began to consider running away, but Mr. Parkland abruptly changed his tack. "Where do you live?"

"Uh…."

"Well do you know where you live or are you lost all the time?" Mr. Parkland asked belligerently.

"I live on the corner of Maple and Centennial." Tony answered.

"So you live on Maple." Mr. Parkland stated.

"Yes." Tony answered, wondering how Mr. Parkland knew that.

"And you take the Press and your father is Thomas Norris." Mr. Parkland went on.

"Yes."

"Say "Yes-sir"."

"Yes-sir." Tony repeated, abashed that he had not answered that way to start with.

"Well, that's a pretty good recommendation. Your Dad always pays his bill on time and never gives any excuses to the delivery boy when he tries to collect. What's your first name?" Mr. Parkland picked up an ink pen from a mug, began to make notes, shoved it into the mug full of pens on his desk and picked up another when he discovered the first didn't work.

"Tony." he answered

"What? I thought your name was Anthony." Mr. Parkland scribbled out something he had already written and replaced it.

"Well, I go by Tony, but my real name is Anthony."

"So which do you want on your pay-check?" Mr. Parkland asked.

"You mean, 'm hired?" Tony had thought from the way Mr. Parkland had talked that he was too ignorant to be hired.

"Well, do you want the job or not?" Mr. Parkland stopped writing on his pad.

"Uh…yes?"

"Is that a question or an answer? I have others that have applied for the position." Mr. Parkland snapped.

"Yes, I want to be a paper boy." Tony answered quickly. And just as quickly threw up his hands to prevent being hit in the face by a wadded up canvas bag that Mr. Parkland threw at him.

"Good. Here's your bag, Junior out on the docks will show you how to fold the papers and here is the collection ring with all your customers listed." Mr. Parkland held out one of the rings of cards with a punch tool hanging from it as well. "Don't lose the hole punch." He admonished. "The Still boys are throwing your route as a favor to me right now. They will take you around once and then you are on your own."

Tony just stood there holding the bag and the ring of cards.

"Hop to it!" Mr. Parkland said and pulled out a new cigarette to light from the old one and began to rummage through papers on his desk. "Move!"

Tony moved.

His first few days on the route were pure misery. The Still twins showed up at his house with the newspapers the next day, and one of them told him "Fetch the ring of customers. The names of the customers that are paid up is organized alphabetically on the ring."

Then the other said, "Throw a paper at each of those houses."

Then together they said, "Did Junior teach you to fold papers?"

"There was nobody left out in the Press loading dock when Mr. Parkland hired me, so I just went home." Tony answered.

Then the twins both folded a paper into a sort of triangle and said, "Fold them like this except on Wednesdays." Then, they went off and left him.

He had looked at the collecting cards on the ring and had surmised from them that his route was on Centennial from Garrison to Baker blvd and on all side streets for two blocks both north and south, plus the hospital and a loop around Hillcrest Drive which he didn't even know how to get on to. He only had forty six papers to throw, but it was plenty.

Not being sure what to do, Tony started walking from his house with the unfolded papers in his bag and he tried to fold them as he walked, but it was windy and made it impossible. His neck was already aching by the time he reached Gentry's corner store at Garrison and Centennial and he sat down on the porch out front to take off his bag. People stared at him as they went in and out the store as he attempted to fold the papers they way the Still brothers had done it. He carefully unfolded one of the papers they had prepared and followed the creases in the paper. When he had half the papers folded, his bag was overflowing. Tony pulled out a white handkerchief from his pocket and blew his nose, running from being out in the cold. There were big black smears left on the handkerchief as he carefully folded it back up to put in his pocket. It was then he noticed that his hands were as black as any he had seen at the Press. Then he saw the front of his jeans were black too, and the cuffs of his coat. What he couldn't see was the black on his face. He wasn't sure what to do, so he went in the store and asked, Mr. Batson, "Could I store the papers here while I go and deliver half?"

"Them Still boys always done that." Lloyd Batson answered from behind the counter . "Didn't they tell you that?"

"No-sir. But I appreciate you letting me leave some papers here." Tony responded with gratitude. "I won't be too long."

Lloyd looked at Tony, and the bag of wadded papers and withheld any comment as Tony left.

Tony looked at the first name on his ring. It started with a W. That couldn't be right, so Tony began to hastily sort through looking for A. There were no cards that the name started with A so he went on to B. It was at this point that he realized he was looking at first names, not last, so he started over. Frank Ames was the first name on the list, and he lived in the eleven-hundred block of Centennial. Tony began to run down the street. After a couple of blocks, he realized he was just at the six hundred block of Centennial. Eleven hundred block was still five blocks away. He slowed to a walk and reconsidered his strategy.

As he stood on the sidewalk in front of the hospital, which took up all of the block on the north side of the street, he heard a voice. He looked over to the north side of the street to see a little old woman holding a shawl around her shoulders glaring angrily at him.

"Are you just going to stand there, or are you going to bring me my paper?" the old woman shouted again.

"Uh…" Tony hesitated and then began to shuffle through his ring of customers looking for any on the six-hundred block of Centennial. Then he found it. The most tattered and marked up card on the entire ring. It had red x's all down one side indicating complaints from that customer. It had non-payment notes from the previous paperboys, and over all of that, there was written in black marker, WATCH OUT! Tony fumbled the cards but managed to see before he dropped them that this house was on his ring and the hole for "April" had been punched, so the customer was paid up.

Tony started to run out into the street, only to be greeted by angry honking from a black Ford sedan turning into the hospital parking lot. When it was clear, Tony ran across the street and pulled out a paper to hand to the old lady. "Here you go Ma'am." He said as he handed her the folded paper and it unfolded itself and scattered pages down the front steps. Tony quickly grabbed up the paper as the old lady looked angrily on.

"Here you are Ma'am." He said as he handed her the disheveled pages.

She pulled back her hands, just as he let go of the paper and again it was scattered on her front steps.

"Don't you try to foist those dirty pages off on me youngster!" the old lady said rudely, "You give me one of those fresh nice papers, like I paid for!"

Tony took another of his badly folded papers from his bag and handed it to the old lady. This time the transfer was complete.

"Well that is not much better." She said with a sniff, looking at the crooked folds distastefully. "Don't you try to cheat me young man. It takes a bigger man than you to cheat LouElla Courtney!"

Mrs. Courtney's irregular acquaintances were perhaps the most varied. She would call and ask the IRS to send out a man to check her taxes. Her taxes were always perfect. She had only one source of income, a trust fund from her father, and only one dependent, herself. Charles Schmidt and Associates oversaw the trust that her father had left and had to deal with her vagaries. The IRS thought for years someone was calling tipping them off, so they always sent someone out, and they hung around Schmidt and Associates taking up time and drinking coffee until they came to the conclusion that everything was fine.

Only once was an irregularity found when she claimed a child named P.C. Courtney as a dependent. This was a ploy to get the IRS man out who had refused to come when she just called in. P.C., it turned out, stood for Pussy Cat. Charles Schmidt and Associates were scolded for letting this slip by. LouElla was insulted in 1959 though, when the IRS sent a woman out to talk with her. Women in government jobs were out of Mrs. Courtney's range of experience.

Compound Interest

Brooks Graves had worked in the courthouse for almost forty years, moving from clerk to Judge. Now he had died, and his family had posted the normal notices in the paper about collecting debts and the transfer of money owed to the estate of Brooks Graves. Charles Schmidt was the executor of his estate, which was fitting since he had been Brooks bookkeeper/accountant and financial advisor most of his life.

There had been almost no bills turned in that Brooks had owed. Brooks had a small bill down at Moe's Market at the corner of Macon and Grand. There was a small charge from Andress Plumbing for a recent stoppage repair at his house, and that was about it, except for the one from old Samuel (Grandpa Sam) Wofford. Sam was the shoeshine "boy" in the lobby of the Jasper County Courthouse. Sam had the chair right next to the elevator and had for as long as Charles Schmidt could remember. In fact, this bill from Sam Wofford was from the very first time Charles had seen Brooks step up into Sam's chair and have his shoes polished.

Brooks had just gotten his new job clerking for old Judge Clark. His mother had dusted and wiped and cleaned on Brooks' brown suit till it looked fine, except that the sleeves were a bit short. The suit had been purchased for Brooks entrance to Law School and Brooks had continued to grow right through graduation. Charles remembered the day well. It had been filled with joy and anticipation. Joy for Brooks, because of his acceptance by Judge Clark to study for the bar while clerking for him, and anticipation since this meant that Brooks would soon be able to marry his long suffering girl, Susan Short.

Charles had been waiting at the top of the courthouse steps with Suzy that morning when Brooks walked up the sidewalk and mounted the steps. He was not looking up, but scuffing his shoes along, and then stopped partway up the steps to rub the top of his shoes agains the back of his pant leg. Susan let out a small gasp when he did that, and Brooks looked up and saw Susan and Charles and broke into one of his huge all-encompassing grins as he ran up to greet us. "What is this?" he asked as he took both of Suzy's white gloved hands in his.

"We have come to wish you Godspeed as you charge into your new endeavor!" she laughed. " No man should start a new job without a grand send-off."

"But, I'm not going anywhere." he answered.

"It's a good thing. Look at those shoes!"

Brooks started to rub his shoes on the back of his pant legs again,"Don't you dare. You get in there and have Grandpa Sam shine up your shoes."

So Charles held the doors open, and Brooks waited for Suzy to step in, then followed her in and across the center of the courthouse, past the civil war cannon and the display from the Great War and over to Sam's chair. William Wainsford was climbing down out of the chair and flipped a dime to Sam as he got on board the elevator. Grandpa Sam caught the dime with a flourish and made it disappear into his cigar box/cash register.

Brooks got in the chair awkwardly that first time, and set his shoes up on the iron stands, then watched with interest as Sam brushed his shoes with one hand and rummaged through his little box of tools to find a rag with dye on it the right hue for Brooks's brown shoes with the other. When he was done, Sam stood back and smiled at the shine and Brooks climbed down from the chair and reached in his pockets. "I uh...... I don't have a dime."

Sam just smiled and said, "It's on me Mr. Brooks sir." and he turned away to put up his tools.

"No!" Suzy jumped in. "You can't do that. Charles, you're an accountant, you just write up a loan paper for Mr. Wofford and you do it up right. Make it compound monthly and prime plus one."

"What?" Brooks said. "What is that?"

"You don't think I just sat around waiting for you to get out of the Army and then become a lawyer do you?" Suzy laughed.

"Well, no, you been working over to the bank." he answered.

And so, Charles wrote a contract on a piece of yellow scratch pad and we all signed it, even Sam's brother who was the elevator operator and Brooks gave it to Sam and then we all rushed off to work.

And now forty years and one month later, Charles was holding the worn yellow contract in his hand, and a little notebook with the figures for every single time Brooks had gotten Sam to clean and shine his shoes. According to Sam, and Sam's nephew Curtis who now worked part days when Sam was just too beat, Brooks had never once paid his shoe shining bill.

Charles had seen Brooks jump in the chair and Sam rush in and do a quick job and Brooks rush off saying, "Just put it on my tab Sam, and remind me to pay that one of these days."

And Sam would answer, "Yessir" and that would be that.

Now, here was Sam and his nephew Curtis, who had helped him up the stairs to Charles's office, waiting for my answer.

"Now Mr. Smit," He always called Charles Mr. Smit, unable to get the full Schmidt out of his mouth without choking on it somehow, "Now Mr. Smit, Mr Graves done give me ceegars every Chrissymas since that first year, and I will deduct them from his bill if you would like."

"Sam, have you been keeping these records ever since nineteen and nineteen?" I was looking through the little notebook he had handed me.

"Yessir, I done just like you showed me." Sam smiled as I looked at the perfectly aligned columns and carefully noted dates and times.

"You asked me about the interest rate every month all that time?" Charles asked, thinking about his quick conversations with Sam over the years as he sat in his chair and had him polish his shoes or boots as the case may be.

"Yessir" Sam smiled, "You was mighty helpful."

"And you learned how to figure compound interest from me?" Charles didn't remember that.

"Oh nosser." He answered quickly, "I learned that from the Mrs. Graves. She done schooled me on that when I wanted to buy me a house all them years ago and was thinkin' of gettin' a loan. I never done it though, after she splained what it really cost. I just saved and bought my little place, cash."

"Well why do you think you should pay for the cigars that Brooks, that is Mr. Graves, gifted to you for Christmas?"

"Well sir, I never was too hip on tobaccer, my Grandpa and Pa always having hands stained and sore from pickin' and workin' tobbaccer fields, that was afore we come here from Kentucky, and everybody in the family chawin or smoking or spitting all the time, sos I trade them ceegars for the newspaper that was always here at my chair. Homer over to the tobacco and news store would give me a years 'scription to the Kansas City Star for them ceegars, and

I traded him every year. It was a good trade for me. I had me a paper to read when it was slow and folks like pickin' it up and readin' while I was a shinin' theys shoes. Many a time a man would say give her the extry shine while I finish this here story, and it would make me another nickel just like that."

"And you are sure the numbers here are correct?" Charles asked, still a little stunned at the results.

"Oh yes sir!" Sam answered proudly. "My boy Charley, the very one that is named after you Mr. Smit, he is a 'prentice countant right there at your firm and he checked the numbers fer me. He thought maybe I shouldn't bring this to you, but after I read that notice in the paper and all about turning in debts owed by Mr. Brooks R. Graves, I figured I best get it done."

"Well, I would certainly trust Charley's work if he checked them." And the amount owed to you by Mr. Graves is," here Charles held the book up and read carefully, "Twelve thousand, eight hundred, seventy-five dollars and ninety-four cents and then point five, four more of a cent?"

"Yessir, though I don't rightly know but what we should just drop that half a penny part." Sam answered. "That there compound interest, it is a 'mazin' thing ain't it."

In 1950 Mrs. Courtney decided to sell her dear departed Daddy's car that had been parked in the carriage shed out behind her house in nineteen and twenty-one. She called her friend Lucien Wainsford about the car, and Lucien talked to her husband William Wainsford II,owner of the local Ford Dealership, about the car and so, one day at lunch time, William and his buddy Oroville "Monty" Montgomery went to Mrs. Courtney's house to look at the car.

Daddy's Car

When they reached the house, LouElla was waiting for them. She took one look at Monty, and said, "You two just walk around beside the house. I'll meet you out back." And she slammed the door in their faces.

"Well, a hell of a thing that is." William said, obviously in favor of leaving, but Monty just shrugged it off.

"We came out here, guess I will go take a look." Monty grinned at Willy, "I reckon the coal dust and holes burnt in my shirt were enough to put her off."

When they got around back, LouElla was waiting. "It's just right out there in back in the carriage house. Here's the key, I reckon you can let yourselves in."

The truth was, LouElla had been out to the carriage house the day before and had been unable to get the big swinging doors open.

William unlocked the big old Schlage lock, which was liberally coated with some kind of grease that smelled to William like rancid fried chicken. Monty lifted the edge of the door and walked it back so it stood ninety degrees open. The first thing that greeted them was stacked lumber. It had been neatly stacked, but the bottom few boards had been lunch for the local termites and the pile now leaned against the other door. Monty pulled the chain to unlatch the top of the door, then reached down and lifted the bar up out of the hole in the concrete floor, then jumped back as the entire pile pushed the door open and fell out into the driveway.

The crashing had barely died down, when the window on the south east corner of Mrs. Courtney's house opened and she shouted, "You just plan on cleaning that mess up Mr. Oroville Montgomery!"

Monty turned to Mrs. Courtney and waved in agreement as William cursed her under his breath. Dust had billowed up when the lumber fell and William's good brown suit was now lighter brown on the front from a liberal coating of dirt and termite poop.

Monty began to move the lumber, re-stacking it half-hazardly off to the side. He was surprised at the heft of the pieces until he realized it was not one by twelve pine decking, as he had supposed on first glance, but was in-stead, five quarter by twelve cherry. As he got down to the bottom few, they were almost entirely consumed by termites. While he had been moving the wood, William had worked the other door aside letting the sun stream in. There was still no car in sight, just a dark green tarp over a shapeless lump. It looked too short to be a car. The bottom of the tarp was rotted off anywhere it reached the ground, and hung in tatters. William and Monty each took what they perceived as a corner and they pulled.

William's side promptly tore off leaving him holding a dirty chunk of canvas that seemed to be covered in raccoon poop. He dropped it, dusted his hands, shrugged and grabbed on again and they both pulled and with a ripping noise from the back of the shed, the bulk of the tarp slid out into the drive as they walked north from the door. What met their gaze was a pair of large headlights with what appeared to be a metal storm window laying across them and right behind them an upside down bathtub. Both stared for a minute or so, moving from side to side to get a better view when suddenly Monty burst out, "By god it's a Stanley Steamer!"

And indeed it was. William Wainsford looked disappointed, but Monty was delighted. "My Grandpa used to tell me about a steamer in town. It spooked the horses and made the dogs howl when the driver would toot the whistle. I bet it was this very car."

"Well my wife expects me to buy this thing from Mrs. Courtney, and I don't want it. People would laugh if I parked it out there with my new Fords." William was disgusted with the idea.

"How much is Mrs. Courtney selling it for?" Monty asked as he squeezed his way around the side of the dark form in the garage.

"Fifty damn dollars." William answered. " I can buy good used cars all day for forty bucks and sell them for eighty. I won't be able to give this thing away."

"I'll buy it." Monty answered immediately.

His willingness to buy made William suspicious, but the thought of the wreck sitting at his dealership and the loss of fifty dollars made his mind up for him. "You can have it."

"One thing, I'll need to use your wrecker." Monty said rubbing a spot clean on the bodywork to expose the dark red paint under the years of grime.

"Sounds good to me." William Wainsford II was pleased to be out from under the obligation to buy the car, and Monty was tickled pink.

So, Monty Montgomery picked up the only decorative item ever present in his shop, a 1911 Stanley Steamer, Model sixty-two.

*LouElla was satisfied with the sale of her Father's car and
even more satisfied that Oroville Montgomery also purchased the
stack of lumber for ten more dollars and the fact that Lucien had
made the deal for the car, gave her the assurance that William
Wainsford II had not cheated her.*

*She found out years later that Oroville had traded his friend
Buck "Red" Feather to build a hutch for Mrs. Montgomery and a
hope chest for his little girl Linda (Lindy to just about everyone) out
of the cherry lumber.*

*She was relieved on the day nearly a week after the first visit,
when Monty closed and locked the doors to the carriage house and
left for the final time, his hauling and moving all completed.*

Monty and the Lathe

Monty Montgomery was a throwback to another age. He
belonged in a setting about one hundred years prior to the time he
lived. His grasp of modern technology went just about as far as he
could knock it with his five-pound hammer. Even back in the early
fifties when he opened his little shop down on the north side of
town, he look like an old timer. Grey hair cut short, black stubble on
his face, thick dark hair on his arms and hands, except where he
was constantly burning it off and thick muscular forearms and huge
biceps. Monty had a physique that would have pleased any body-
builder and strength to please any Olympic weightlifter. He had a
shop in a big old building that may have started life as a barn, but
had been built on to and changed so often it was unrecognizable as

anything other than a conglomeration of sheds. The front door was hinged slabs of wood, inset into large barn doors that could be rolled aside for access to the inside or for ventilation if the weather was warm. It had a very crude hand painted sign on it that said Monty's Wel. The other half of "welding" had been broken off. He once had a board with his hours painted on it but he had found it restrictive and had painted over it with another sign that said "Open when I'm here. Closed when I'm not." Most folks couldn't read the lettering through all the coal soot. The central part of the building was two stories high with the loft floor removed. This was the room where the forge was and had a dark brick floor that was almost black from the soot, coal, clinkers, and metal chips. Huge beams crossed overhead about ten feet high supporting the hood over his forge and crude hooks holding hardware from generations of work. Scrap metal was piled everywhere with bins full of horseshoes, sickle knives, plow knives, rivets and miscellaneous junk. Mostly junk. There was a stall in the back where a horse that needed shoeing could be kept while he was working on something else, but the only way in was through his shop. There was a casement window on the back of the stall with no screen. He pitched the leftovers from the horses out into the yard behind his shop until Stinky Randall complained, then he had to start carrying the horses little gifts out through the front of the shop to dispose of them. That was a lot of trouble so that only got done when he couldn't get the stall door closed any more, therefore the shop always smelled of a horse stall, even when there hadn't been a horse in the place for months. There were two windows way up high covered with cobwebs and flyspecks so only a little yellow light came in. he would climb up the framing of the barn in late spring and swing the windows back and wire them in place. In summer there were always barn swallows going in and out. Monty liked the sounds they made, and and that they ate flying bugs, so figured he could deal with the messes under their nests. More light came in around the big metal flue that went up from the hood over his forge. Light, rain, snow, and birds each came in during the appropriate seasons. When it rained there would be a little river running out the front of the shop through the big rolling doors. It was directed on it's course by a little ditch that was formed into the brick. The gutter had originally been in the barn floor for other purposes but it served Monty admirably. He kept his quenching tank over the little ditch, so any overflow would run out the door and not leave his floor muddy. When he tossed a big piece of smoking, red hot, iron into the tank, the water would surge out across the floor, then gather in little rivulets and run out the front of his shop. It made a little rusty river for blocks every time he replaced the water in the tank.

Monty had a phone once, but besides the monthly bill, it cost him a couple of plow knives when somebody called and he burnt them in his forge. Then one of the horses he was shoeing got fractious and mashed it off the wall and Monty had the phone company pick it up and disconnect it. The same horse also stomped two of Monty's toes off. Old Doc Summers went over to Monty's shop to sew his foot up. Then Monty went back to work. He always packed newspaper in his boot where his toes should have been, and he claimed he never missed them. His wife didn't like him to rub his foot on her in bed after that though. In the summer Monty would get up early and go down to his shop, roll the big front doors aside, and fire up the forge. He then would set a big pot with coffee and water mixed in it along side the fire until it boiled, then set the pot alongside the flue on a shelf he had welded there to keep his coffee hot. In the winter, the doors stayed closed, but the rest of his routine stayed the same. If the winds were out of the north, the smell of coal from the forge would travel uptown to the square, eventually spreading clear across town. By the end of the day the coffee would be so strong you could have patched the street with it. Many an unwary customer was given a cup of this concoction and felt compelled to drink it because Monty was standing there watching them. It only took one time to learn to refuse coffee when Monty offered, unless it was very early in the morning.

In nineteen fifty-eight Monty decided to invest in a WWI vintage engine lathe that a US Government surplus store was selling. He had seen the advertisement in the Popular Mechanics magazine that Ron Yates had at his barber shop. Monty had written the company and after a few months and several letters changing hands, Monty's lathe was on its way to Carthage from Leavenworth Kansas on a train car. Monty solicited the help of Mark Feckles, and his wrecker, to haul the big lathe to his shop. Monty had cleaned out the lean-to on the south side of his shop, rolling his prized Steamer out of it's space and across to the old horse stall, and re-covering it with the quilt and the big tarp to keep it clean. He needed the room in the lean-to for the lathe to sit in. He even put an electric light in the horse stall when he moved the old Stanley Steamer that he had drug in from LouElla Cortney's place eight years before. He needed the light for when he would get around to repairing the beautiful old car to run, rather than just keeping it shined up.

The first problem came when the train came in. The train crew unhooked the flatcar the lathe was on, and rolled it onto a siding. Martin MacDonald down at the railroad tried to find a phone number for Monty. He planned to call in order to inform Monty his load had arrived, but couldn't find a number, so he decided to go by Monty's shop after work and tell him that his lathe had arrived. Then a call came in that there was a derailment on a siding out on the south end of town that had the main line blocked. It was raining cats and dogs and Martin was going to be forced to call in the emergency repair crew. So telling Monty about the lathe was relegated to the back burner and Martin worked around the clock with his crew to get the tracks cleared and repaired.

Two days later, on the way to the donut shop, Martin stopped by the blacksmith shop to see Monty. "Mornin' Monty! Thought I would drop by and tell you your machine was in. It's down on the far west siding. It's covered by a big tarp and there is a couple of big crates with it."

"Thanks Martin." Monty stopped his hammering for a bit to respond. "I got Mark Feckles to move it for me."

"It's pretty big." Martin was thinking about Mark Feckles winch truck compared to the lathe.

"Yup." Monty answered and began to whang away at the big piece of iron on his anvil.

It was still raining the next morning, when Monty rousted out Mark Feckles and went to the train depot to pick the lathe up. Mark had a '48 Ford two-ton truck with a winch on back. It was army surplus too but a good deal more recent than the lathe, though in considerably rougher condition. The old Ford had been rolled over and all the windows knocked out. Then Mark had cut the doors off. He dropped a tree on it soon after that, so then he went to work and had Monty weld two-inch pipe all over the top and sides. He had a headache for a week the next time he dropped a tree on the roof of his truck. A branch came through the roof between the bars, and popped him on the noggin. So then he planned to go to Monty to have plate welded on the top and hardware cloth welded in where the windshield and the back window had been. Monty had been closed up though, so Mark went to his buddy Mac Jones at the hardware store, and they pulled out the new arc welder from the store and learned how to use it together. His truck was now an art form all it's own.

It was still raining as Mark pulled into the train station. He spotted Monty several hundred yards down the gravel track bed with his head under a tarpaulin that covered a large lump on a flatcar. Mark jammed his truck into low range and roared down the side of the track splashing mud and water all over himself in the process. It was late spring, and warm and Mark didn't really mind.

Monty walked around the lathe cutting the hemp twine that held the tarp and drug it aside, and found that the crew that had loaded the lathe had left the big steel rings bolted to the lathe, so he motioned for Mark to back up to the train car.

Mark left the comparative dry of the truck and joined Monty in the steady rain. "What you need Monty?" He asked, looking at the size of the lathe and estimating it's weight in his head.

"A couple of cables and a clevis should do the job."

"I ain't got any cable but on the winch." Mark answered.

Monty considered that problem and came to a decision, "Well if you got enough cable, I'll just loop it through the rings on the lathe and hook it to itself."

It sounded simple. It even looked simple. Mark let some slack into the cable. Monty ran the cable hook through one ring then through the other ring at the other end of the lathe, and hooked it back to itself. He motioned to Mark standing at the controls on the driver side of the truck, and Mark started the winch. First the cable slipped causing Monty to take a flying leap off the flatcar into the ditch on the siding. Then when the cable slack was all taken up the truck sagged, and the train car raised up as the weight of the lathe was taken up. The winch wasn't tall enough to lift the big machine over the lip on the edge of the flatcar.

The solution was to drag the lathe off the flatcar one end at a time. Monty climbed back up, unhooked the cable then re-hooked it to the light end of the lathe, Mark revved up the wrecker and drug the end of the lathe over the edge of the flatcar. Four things happened at once, or nearly at once. The front of the truck jumped up off the ground, the flatcar tipped down on the side the lathe was on, Monty went for another swim in the mud and the lathe joined him on the ground. Mark's fist reaction was to run when the truck reared up so, left to it's own devices, the truck was still pulling itself up toward the sky, the old V8 screaming in protest. If the clutch had not been so bad the truck would have pulled itself over. As it was it would rear up until the front wheels were about four feet off the ground, then the clutch would slip and scream, smoke would fly and then the truck would lurch back down to the ground. It went through this cycle four times before Monty caught hold of the frame of the cab as it lurched down and dove into the passenger door and turned off the key. As luck would have it was near the top of one of it's lifting cycles when he got the engine turned off, so when he turned the key the engine took off backwards lurching down as the weight of the truck unwound the cable. When it hit bottom, it threw Monty back out the door of the truck and back into the mud. The lathe was down off the train-car, upright, though wet and muddy, but seemingly undamaged. Mark had had enough. He unhooked the cable, started the truck, wound the slack back up onto the winch, and spewed mud as he roared out of the train-yard. Monty was still trying to get the mud out of his eyes and ears when Mark's truck bounced over the bridge and out of sight.

Martin was coming in from the donut shop as Mark went out of the yard. Martin was feeling mellow. He had enjoyed a full nights sleep with no emergencies the night before. The morning shift was quiet so far. The donuts had been good, the coffee fresh and the skies were clearing after the downpour the previous six days. All was well. He didn't even notice Mark roaring out of the train-yard, but he did notice Monty or at least it looked like Monty, standing next to a big piece of machinery. Both appeared to be coated generously with the slime flowing down the ditch by the siding. Martin cruised his pickup on down to the loading ramp where the crew was relaxing under the eaves of the old original depot. It was now the crew office/lounge. When he got there he was invited to join the rest of the boys and watch the show. Monty handed out the donuts, then the boys filled him in on the thirty minutes that he had been gone. About the time Martin finished another cup of coffee, Monty had enough mud off of his head to see where he was going and started up to the old depot. Some of the boys looked uncomfortable and got up and headed out to the rigs to move out for ditch cleanup. Some of the others that didn't even know Monty, took the hint, and cleared out too, leaving just Martin and Jake King. Jake was ready to retire and manned the office when the crew was out on the track. It took Monty a few minutes to get up to the building so Martin went inside to check on something, anything, and left Jake out to greet him and find out when he was moving the lathe.

Monty had cooled down a little by now, and was almost civil to Jake. "Can I use your phone?"

"Sure, let me hand you the hand-piece and I'll dial for you. No need to track all over the office." Jake went in and pulled out the hand-piece on the phone. It had a long cord on it so someone talking could stand outside and look down the track. "What's your number?"

Monty didn't know anyone's phone number by memory. "Can you look up Feckles Wrecker service and dial that?"

"Sure Monty. Give me a minute." Jake grabbed the phone book and looked up the number and dialed it, and then stood outside the thin partition wall of the outer office to hear what Monty was going to say.

The first call was a short one. As soon as Mark Feckles answered the phone Monty started screaming and Mark terminated that conversation by hanging up.

"Could I borrow your phone book please?" Monty said to Jake and Jake grabbed it up and took it out to Monty.

Then Monty started going down the list of wreckers in the phone book and giving Jake the numbers to dial. The first two refused on the grounds that their trucks were too small. The next one hung up when they heard who it was calling. The next number was busy. Coffee shop talk the next day confirmed what Monty was beginning to suspect. Mark was one phone number ahead of him calling the other wrecker owners. And Monty had just called the last one in the yellow pages.

Jake was in danger of busting a gut holding in his laughter, when Monty handed him the phone and stormed out. As he stomped down the ramp and started toward the lathe he discovered the gremlins had been at work. The lathe had now sunk on one corner and tipped over, submerging the loading hooks in a foot of muddy water. The water swirled around the lathe on its way toward the big drainage ditch on the north end of the train-yard. Monty was defeated. He didn't even have a way to get home other than walking. His wife had dropped him off at the train yard so he could ride back on the wrecker with the lathe. So, he started to walk.

Martin had left the old depot and gone out to the rail-yard garage. He had pulled in a couple of men from the track and was busy loading equipment onto the track moving truck. As soon as Monty was out of sight, Martin and the crew put the truck on the track, roared out to the lathe, pushed the flatcar back, and hooked onto the lathe. The lathe was a small load for the big track hauler and with a minimum of fuss the lathe was set on the track carrier and boomed down. In a few minutes, the big crates full of machine tools joined the lathe.

Martin and the boys drove down the tracks to a crossing about two blocks from Monty's shop, pulled up the track wheels and drove up to Monty's shop. Martin then rolled back the doors to Monty's shop, and he and the boys put the lathe on big rail moving dollies and rolled it into the lean-to next to the big main shop and gently lowered it into place, where for many years a Stanley Steamer had resided. Then they loaded the big wood crates to the floor just inside the doors, and Martin and the boys pulled the doors shut, and rushed down the block to watch. They got out of sight, just as Monty rounded the corner from the north, walking along with a determined stride.

When Monty walked in through the small door, he stopped and just stood there until the wind caught the door and blew it back shut against him, nearly knocking him down. Martin and the boys started to walk back toward the shop to yell, "Surprise!" when there was a tremendous crash from the lean-to. Billows of dust blew out around the rock foundation of the little room addition and the walls sagged inward. The boys and Martin decided to leave. Monty had been the straw that broke the camels back. The floor of his lean-to had fallen in. Unlike the central part of the shop, the little addition had a wooden floor framed up with two by eights. The lathe now sat in the dirt in the crawlspace below the remaining floor, on its side. Monty was lying next to it. No one ever told him how the lathe got to his shop, but he knew. He went home and didn't open up again for three days.

Vacuum cleaner salesman passed the word down the grapevine that Mrs. Courtney was one to avoid, after a couple of them vacuumed her entire house as a demonstration of their machines superiority.

LouElla had an entire shelf with encyclopedias of various years, the A volume only. These were given away as samples to entice people to buy the whole set. She never did. Her favorite part of the encyclopedia was "animals", and that was always in the first volume. Why waste money for some volumes she might not ever use? One of her greatest triumphs was convincing one salesman to give her a B volume one year.

Trash men were a regular part of her week. Tuesday was her day for years, back when trash was hauled in the back of a '39 Plymouth, by a family from the north side of town. She knew how to deal with these trash collectors. They were rather unsavory looking and smelling. Randall was the family name. Father, grandfather, brothers, uncles, sisters, mothers, and grandmothers were all roughly the same size and shape, and wore each others clothing interchangeably. Even in the summer at least three shirts and a couple of pairs of pants were in vogue with the Randalls. Word among the school kids was that the Randalls ate people. Mrs. Courtney never went for this theory. The Randalls picked up trash until 1969 when the city contracted with a regular trash service.

Stinky's Day

The day started out like so many others that Stinky didn't notice anything out of the ordinary. He lay on his back, warm under the big army blanket and the old wedding quilt, listening and looking. There were dim frames of light, outlined in random patterns, where windows had been patched, boarded, card-boarded, and stuffed full of rags in a very ineffectual attempt to separate the weather outdoors from the weather indoors, showing the dim glow of predawn. He studied the dark outlines of the whole family, four generations worth, all sleeping on the floor, except Troy in the big easy chair. (It was his turn.) Of course He and Dora (Ma to everyone else) got the bed. It was his house. When Stinky woke some mornings, he wondered if the bed was better than the floor, what with his multitudinous aches and pains, but not this day. He felt fine.

Grumbles, moans and finally shouts emanated from the forms on the floor as Grandma stepped on folks on her way to the back door and out to the outhouse. It was late March. The weather had warmed up a little, and the thunder pot had been taken out of the closet, the first ritual of spring at the Randall house.

The newest baby of Marcia's began to whimper in his basket where he slept. Stinky thought about that basket a minute, contemplating all the babies that had slept in it since he had found it in the trash up on Grand only two or three months after he and Dora got married. He lost count at around twenty-seven kids, counting all his kids and grandkids and now a couple of great-grandkids. Stinky sat up on the edge of the bed and lit the small kerosene lantern sitting on a hogshead that served as his night table, careful of the cracked globe. When the light sputtered to life, he stepped across the room, and gently picked up the complaining baby, hugging him tight, and handed him over to Marcia who slid him up under her coat, which she was sleeping in, and both baby and his Momma promptly went back to sleep.

It looked like Dora had left beans on the stove, but from how cold it was in the room it was obvious the fire had gone out, so Stinky, now fully awake, laced up his boots, fished his false teeth out of their Noxema bottle he kept them in at night, poked them in his mouth, put an old leather cap with big furry brim and ear flaps that snapped up, on his head, and was ready to face the world.

Jonas, Stinky's youngest, hadn't come home the night before but Stinky had not noticed till he took inventory of the sleeping forms. "Off to his brother's place again." he thought. "Lord he loves all that junk out at his brother's barn, but he'll show up for the route. This is his day." Stinky stuffed a wad of stained rags into the kitchen range and looked around for a match. He found one broken kitchen match stuck in the cast iron match holder on the wall. The rags he had stuffed into the stove, must have had something besides just dirt and grease on them. When Stinky lit them, the flames whooshed up, sizzling his beard and eyebrows. The rags burned cheerfully a moment, then fizzled out.

"Heck." Stinky said under his breath. For a minute he considered his predicament. "Beans is fine cold for breakfast. Beans only need to be hot for supper." Stinky mused aloud, but no one paid him any mind.

Grandma came back in and sat in the rocker by the stove waiting to get warm. It was a failure, so she shuffled back across the room again, stumbling through the sleeping folks and snuggled up to a big old redbone hound that had occupied her mat in the corner during her absence. After some negotiations, both were comfortable and drifted back off to sleep.

Stinky decided for sure. He could eat cold beans for breakfast. He found a mostly clean spoon, polished it clean with his thumb, lifted the lid of the big cast iron pot and shoveled a few beans out on a heavy stoneware plate. Even cold, the pleasing smell of pork rind and onion drifted up from the pot. "Yes sir" he thought, "beans cold for breakfast is just fine." But he missed his coffee. Coffee had to have hot water. Hot water meant a fire. The fire had scorched his face and gone out, but he wanted coffee and coffee took hot water. Stinky thought it all out while he finished his beans, then happened to glance out the back window and saw a light at Oroville "Monty" Montgomery's shop. He couldn't tell if there was smoke coming out of the flue or not, but he knew Monty's habits. Monty wouldn't wait long to fire up the forge, make some coffee, and start banging away at something. Stinky found a china teacup in a bookshelf. It had little red flowers all around it's base, and a gold plated rim and no handle. He took it, remembering that Monty only seemed to have one mug over to the blacksmith shop. Stinky carefully worked his way through the sleeping forms, the hound watched his progress, but was not interested enough to get up and follow. Stinky blew out the little lantern, snugged his coat up a bit, and set off.

He pried open his front door, and stepped out into the brisk pre-dawn air. It was cold, but to Stinky's eye, the day held promise. Long stripes of pale white, originating at one point in the east and spreading like a folded paper fan, were lining the sky, and all but the brightest stars were now hidden. He stepped out purposefully, looking at the cup in his hand as he went. It looked a little dirty, even in the bad light, so Stinky wiped it out with his shirttail as he made his way around the block to the front of Monty's Blacksmith Shop.

Monty was savoring the morning. He had walked down to the shop from his house east of the square, as he did every morning, and was feeling the cold by the time he reached there. He lit the big lantern next to his forge, feeling no need to turn on the electricity until he had work to do. Kerosene light was good enough for making morning coffee. "No need to add to that electric bill 'till he had to." He mused. He slowly began stepping on the low wooden handle that protruded out in front of his forge. It was attached to the big bellows by way of chains and levers. The bellows sat to the back of his brick forge and would push air into the fire when he stepped down on the lever. When he lifted his foot up off the lever, the counter weight would go back down, pulling the bellows open, the bellows sucking in air as it expanded. He would then step down again, gently pushing more air into the pile of coal and coke in the center of his forge. The bellows wheezed a little as air escaped from a small leak in the leather, but not enough to warrant replacing it. Besides, he thought, "I might step up to a hand crank or maybe even an electric forge blower one of these days." Sparks leapt up from the seemingly cold forge, spangling the darkness with bright orange, red and white sparks. He slowly added coal to the fire, white flames lighting the forge, the hood, and his face. The heat felt great. A few more slow steady pumps of the bellows and then Monty pulled down the big metal coffee pot from it's shelf, poured the contents out on the brick floor as he walked to the pump out back. A few strokes of the pump and water gushed into the pot, sloshing away the coffee grounds from the day before, or at least some of them. Monty filled the pot up to the bottom of the spout with fresh cold water. Inside he stepped on the tread of the bellows a few more times to boost up the fire, set the pot down next to the fire, and went to the old dilapidated kitchen cabinet by the back door where he kept his cups, coffee, a few kitchen utensils and old

"Farrier" magazines all in a confusion. He couldn't find his coffee spoon so he picked up a coffee can lid and bent it into a sort of scoop. Then he found that the tin he stored his coffee in was empty, the spoon rattling around in the bottom of the tin, so feeling good for being forward looking, he pulled out a brand new can of MFA coffee that had been on his shelf for at least fifteen years, just in case he ran out before he thought to buy more. There was no little key on the can lid. There wasn't even a tab to roll the little sealing band up with. This can needed a can opener. "Who would have thunk it?" He muttered to himself. "A can of coffee with no opener."

Monty went to his workbench pulled out his hacksaw and started in on the side of the can just below the rim. The can hissed relieving the vacuum in the can and the smell of fresh coffee escaped into the morning air. About an inch into the can he realized the saw was making lots of little steel shavings and they were getting into the coffee. He stopped sawing, clamped the can in the vice and grabbed the lid with some forge tongs and pulled. The tin can ripped satisfactorily then stopped. Monty gave the can lid one more good pull and the can exploded blowing coffee all over the floor, the vice, the bench, and Monty. Monty noticed with some surprise how pretty the flames were that flew up from the forge when ground coffee was sprinkled in the glowing coals. In the bottom of the now ripped in half coffee can was just enough clean coffee to make a pot full. Monty loaded the clean coffee into the coffee pot, stepped on the bellows handle a couple more times, set the pot right on the edge of the forge, almost into the fire, then started cleaning up the mess. He bent the can back into shape. His big hard hands squeezing the tin back into a semblance of it's original can shape with ease. He found a scrap newspaper in the trash and put it inside the can as a liner, not thinking that he had used the paper to catch fish scales when he cleaned some bass he had caught the week before. Having repaired the battered container, he began to sweep up the scattered coffee from the bench, the brick floor, and the stone fire-box of his forge. Just as he had the can almost full, the scrap metal hanging on a cable on his front door rattled to signify someone was there. Stinky Randall had arrived.

Monty didn't mind Stinky too much in the middle of summer. That time of year all Monty's shop doors, and the big upper loft doors were open and you could get up-wind of Stinky. Monty really didn't mind Stinky in mid winter either, 'cause Stinky mellowed out some through the cold weather. In spring and fall though, he was a little hard to take. The shop didn't leak air quite fast enough to make it comfortable to breath with Stinky in there. You could always hope Stinky wouldn't stay long or that he might have fallen in the river again while fishing, and therefore have gotten an impromptu bath.

"Monty. You got any coffee? My stove is out." Stinky didn't believe in unnecessary preliminaries.

"Let me check it out Stinky. We'll see if it's ready." Monty set the can of sweepings down and went to the forge. A little listen and he could hear the coffee boiling in the pot. "Step over here Stinky and have a cup. Fresh brewed."

Monty picked up the big porcelain-coated steel pot by the handle and poured Stinky some coffee. He shook the pot a bit to make sure the grounds were stirred up and that Stinky got his share. Monty got himself a mug and then, carefully, after allowing the grounds to settle, poured himself a cup. Stinky slurped hungrily at his coffee from the little china cup, never noticing the grounds swirling around thick in the bottom. He finished one cup off and picked up the pot to pour himself another. The handle blistered his hand almost immediately and he set the pot down with a crash, rattling the lid off onto the forge. Monty grabbed up the lid, and set it back on the pot.

Stinky said "Hot"

Monty said "Yeah."

Stinky pulled out a rag from his pocket and held it on his hand a moment then started to pick up the pot again using the rag for a pot holder. Monty eyed the rag for a second, determined its origin as being underwear and grabbed the pot out of Stinky's reach and poured Stinky's coffee for him. Monty's logic told him, if Stinky was using underwear for a handkerchief, it must have been worn out by someone else and discarded, before Stinky got it. Then it was worn some more by whichever Randall family member or members it most closely fitted and then was relegated to handkerchief status. Monty didn't mind his own dirt. Stinky's dirt was something else.

Stinky eyed his scorched hand, then Monty's big calloused fist. "'Bliged Monty." Stinky mumbled and headed for Monty's front door.

"Want that can of coffee Stinky?" Monty pointed to the can of sweepings in the split can, "I busted the can."

"Sure. Much 'bliged." Now that Stinky thought about it, he had been out of coffee since yesterday noon. He went out the front door and Monty was relieved of trying to hold his nose, without looking like he was.

As Stinky's passed around the corner and out of sight, Monty held a clean hanky over his face, threw open the big double front doors, their hinges protesting at being moved from their winter position, and stood by the forge to stay warm, while his shop aired out.

Stinky went back around the corner to his house, holding his hand against the cool metal of the coffee can and slurping the last of his coffee from the handleless cup. He went around back of his house where he set his coffee can and cup on the bench next to the rain-barrel, broke the glaze of ice off the top of the water, and dipped his burnt hand in to cool it. He wondered as he went to the back door if Jonas had come home and if Dora was ready to go.

The back door didn't fit well. The old back door had broken in two when one of the kids had slammed it. This new door was from a Junior Randall remodel job and was about four inches too short. Junior had fixed the door by putting a board across the top, but Stinky kept knocking his head on it, so Junior, being the good nephew he was, had come back and hung the door up at the regular height and built up a stack of two-by-fours on the floor to take up the extra space. As Stinky went in the back door, he automatically ducked his head, but then tripped on the tall sill and sprawled out in the kitchen floor. He landed on the hound, which had objected to grandma, and had moved to a spot just beyond the swing of the back door.

The hound had just been dreaming about a traumatic experience he once had. The hound and Jonas had been hunting out west of town when they came upon a circus train. Unloading from the train were colorful wagons, some with wild animals in them. The circus was preparing for a parade the next day. Jonas had to see, and had pulled the poor hound along with him on a hank of rope. Snakes behind glass, an alligator with a portable

67

swimming pool, monkeys and zebras (though the stripes seemed to be running on one of the Zebras and it looked suspiciously like a painted donkey.) At one point Jonas pulled that poor dog right up to a bear cage and let him have a good look. The bear didn't care, but it gave the hound nightmares.

When Stinky fell on him, the startled hound jumped up and bit Stinky on the back of his head. The hound got a mouth full of the big ugly cap Stinky had on and shook it for all he was worth. Stinky crawled away from the slavering, snarling, dog wondering what in the world was wrong with the dog and if maybe, if he had a bullet, he might ought to shoot him. The dog suspended his attack after a moment, smelled the cap and stalked off to the other side of the room and lay down. He watched the cap for a few seconds then got back up, stretched, and went out the back door, which was still standing open. The hound marked his regular spots, the outhouse, the rain barrel, the back gate, the remains of the back fence, and the back of Monty's shop, then crawled under the wood shed and went to sleep. He never dreamed of bears again. He had met his bear and it was his.

Stinky watched the dog leave the room, and got up and closed the door. Dora was gone from the bed so she was up, "Probably out in the front room changing out of her nightdress" he thought, though he didn't hear her. Looking at the cold cookstove, he remembered the coffee, and went back out the back door stepping carefully over the tall threshold and over to the rain barrel where he had left it.

"Must o' splashed water on the coffee when I cooled off my hand." He thought idly as he noticed the drips on the can. He entered the kitchen by the back door, carefully avoiding the tall sill and watching for the hound, thinking he might have come back in.

He stopped just inside the door and stood wondering where to store the coffee. About that time Stinky's grandson, David Jr., who had just been potty trained at the tender age of four, ran out of the front room and out the back door knocking the coffee can out of Stinky's hand with his head. David Jr. was out for an exciting new adventure, a visit to the outhouse. Half of the coffee stayed in the can and half spilled out on the well-trodden floor. Stinky looked at the coffee, then at the can, sighed and scraped most of the coffee up off the floor and back into the can. He unloaded the contents of a three legged kitchen chair, climbed cautiously up on it and set the coffee high up on a shelf where he used to keep his hard liquor, at least when he had some. Stinky had lost the taste for it shortly after his marriage, when he found that Dora disapproved. The can just barely fit, and scraped on the ceiling as Stinky forced it into the space, knocking off the accumulation of years onto the top of the coffee. A spider lost a web that had been in the spider family for untold generations when the can destroyed it.

Stinky made a trip to the outhouse where he found David Jr.'s aim not to be very well developed, so he pushed the droplets off the wooden seat and made himself comfortable.

When Stinky finished his business in the outhouse, including another quick swipe with a page from Sears catalogue at the mess David Jr. had left, he went around front of his house to check the oil in the truck.

The truck was a black and orange thirty-nine, one and a half ton, Dodge. The orange was exclusive to the right front fender, which had been replaced before Stinky had owned the truck. It had a flat wooden bed, much patched and stake sides with timbers of various dimensions, nailed or wired onto the uprights. The top of the truck cab had been steel, when it was new. The center sheet metal had been chopped out, for some project, and now the truck cab was roofed with wood, adorned with red plaid linoleum. (Another Junior Randall remodel cast-off.) There was trash two foot deep in the bed of the truck from previous loads, which made footing treacherous. Stinky opened the right hand hood by unwinding the bailing wire latch, then propped it up with the end of a broken crutch kept wedged in front of the radiator just for that purpose. He retrieved a glass, gallon-jug from behind the seat on the passenger side where he kept his stash of oil. He collected the precious engine oil out of the trash he picked up, strained it through a rag, and used it in his truck, and to light fires, and to waterproof his house. The old flathead six Chrysler engine ran like a top most of the time, unless it was raining hard and the distributor cap got wet enough to wash the chewing gum insulator off. The gum sealed a crack in the cap perfectly until the rain got really heavy or Stinky drove through a big puddle too fast. Stinky had learned not to drive through puddles too fast, not because of the gum on the distributor cap, but because the brakes, which were poor at best, didn't work at all when wet. Stinky checked the dipstick, didn't see any oil on it and poured part of the jug of oil into the engine. He also went around to the other side of the truck and poured some of the oil into the big oil bath air filter and dumped a little in the generator "oil here" holes.

Dora, all dressed and back in the kitchen, sat on the three legged chair waiting for Stinky. This was her day to drive the truck, while Jonas and Stinky rode the tailgate. Pretty soon, she realized Stinky wasn't coming back in the house, and came out and sat in the truck smoking the first of a continuous string of cigarettes. She smoked "roll your owns" most of the time. She made them with pages from a book Stinky had found at the dump. It had very thin, almost translucent pages covered with mathematical formulas and writing in German. Jonas had found the math book and an old German Bible together in a cardboard box at the dump. Dora would sit evenings and tear up the butts of cigarettes she took from the trash at houses where folks smoked store bought cigarettes. She would sort them out, peel them open and save the tobacco. She would carefully cut the pages of the math book into little squares just the right size. She kept an old Prince Albert can and paper wrapper package so folks wouldn't know. It never occurred to her that folks would notice that her cigarettes had printing on them. Dora had wanted to cut up the old German Bible too, for her cigarette papers, but Jonas talked her out of it.

"After all," She had said, "ain't nobody in this family can read no German, and if we was to get caught with a German book, they would think we was spies." She had looked at Jonas and Stinky suspiciously, knowing she was no spy, but not so sure about Jonas and Stinky.

"We ain't spies Ma," Jonas had assured her, "We founded it in the trash like we said, and we don't figure spies would cut up their own books for cigarette papers, but we ain't gonna cut up no Bible, even if it is in some heathen language. It would put a curse on the family sure."

So Dora had hid the Bible in the attic and was always on the look-out for government agents and a new book with thin paper. She decided she wouldn't chop up that old Bible even if she had to smoke cigarettes rolled in slick old Reader's Digests. Dora didn't want anything bad to happen to her family.

Stinky continued his morning maintenance on the truck by going around and checking all six tires. He checked the pressure with the same broken crutch he used to prop open the engine hoods. A thump from the crutch and Stinky could tell within five pounds or so how much air was in the tires and if he needed to stop up at the Standard Station where he bought gasoline to air them up. "Just the inside tire on the left a little low today." He said as he put the crutch back in its place.

After putting up his universal tool, Stinky had gone around back to see if his wiring job to the one lone tail-light was still holding, when he noticed something. "Dora did you see this coat in the back of the truck?" He was peering over the wooden tailgate at a partly buried plaid coat. "It don't look like trash."

Dora climbed out of the truck and looked through an opening in the side of the truck. " A coat."

"Yeah a coat. You seen it afore?" Stinky asked as he poked at it with a loose slat from the side of the truck.

"Maybe" Dora wasn't sure.

Stinky clambered up into the back of the truck raking trash off the home-made tailgate as he climbed in. He went to pull the coat up out of the trash and something jerked against his leg. The summer before there had been a big snake in the trash can behind the Shirley Potter's house and Stinky was a bit jumpy after that. In his panic to escape this apparently large snake in his truck, he threw himself backwards, catching on the tail board and falling head down out the back of the truck. His left pant leg caught on a protruding bolt and arrested his plunge just before his head hit the ground. This left him hanging upside down by one leg.

"What you doin' Pa?" It was Jonas standing in the back of the truck.

"It was Jonas's coat Pa." Dora commented, and got back in the truck.

"Unhook my leg boy." Stinky was trying to pull himself up by the back edge of the bed but every time he did his hands would slip in the trash and drop him again, his head getting closer to the concrete of the street every time

"You want loose Pa?" Jonas caught on fast.

"Yeah Jonas. Let me loose." Stinky would be patient with the boy he thought, since his cards didn't add up to a full deck.

Jonas yanked Stinky's pant leg loose and Stinky crumpled into a pile at the back of the truck. It was his dog-chewed hat saved him from skinning his head. "Good thing that hound hadn't et 'er clear up." He mused as he slapped the cap back on his head, dusted off his clothes, then glared at Jonas. "I thought you was a snake boy." He said, retying his clothesline belt and pulling up his two pairs of britches.

"I ain't no snake Pa. I ain't as skinny as a snake. I don't have no face like a snake neither. Emmett James, now he sorter looks like a snake, Pa, but I don't look like no snake. A ox maybe. Teacher Reynolds said oncet when I wasn't s'posed to hear that I was a ox. She never said nothin' 'bout a snake. I don't look like a snake do I Pa?" Jonas had climbed down from the truck and was earnestly studying his reflection in the broken drivers side mirror. "Snakes got no hair Pa. I got hair. Snakes slither. Do I slither Pa?"

"Get in the truck boy." Stinky was in the cab behind the wheel with the key on.

"OK pa. Don't call me no snake Pa. I don't think I like snakes Pa. 'Cept green snakes and garter snakes and ring necks and black snakes if they ain't too big."

"Let's go boy."

"OK pa." Jonas just stood there by the driver door.

"What was you doin' back there anyway?" It finally occurred to Stinky to ask.

"Well you wasn't out here when I come from Leopold's house and soes I just went and layed down in the truck so as not to miss you, and I was cold so I covereded up with them papers and stuff." Jonas explained, "Did you know you can smell ink on them papers when you cover your head with it?"

"Pull out the board boy." Stinky usually parked the truck on the hill just west of their house. Mornings someone pulled out the board, and when Stinky put in the clutch, the truck coasted down the hill. When he had a little speed built up, he would put it in second gear, pull the choke, give it some gas, pop the clutch, and off he'd go. No worries about cranking (he had lost the hand crank anyway) or a battery being dead. "A hill is always better than a battery." He always said, and added "Hills don't burn holes in your clothes." He had learned this lesson the hard way when someone had thrown a big old lead-acid radio battery in the trash and he had drug it out of the truck and spilled the contents on his lap.

Jonas pulled out the board from in front of the back tire and watched as Stinky coasted down the hill. The truck rolled along a few feet, lurched and jerked as Stinky let out the clutch. The tires let out a little squawk and then with a big backfire and a mighty roar, the engine caught. Stinky turned right at the bottom of the hill and his door came open. He was leaning on the door on account of the frost on the windshield and he came right out with the door. His left arm was outside the door through the window. His left foot was hopping along the ground as fast as it could hop. His right hand had hold of the steering wheel and his right foot was caught between the throttle and the brake pedal. He went south about twenty feet like this then ran up the curb along the side of Lawson's grocery warehouse, the truck hitting the curb shook his right hand loose from the steering wheel, so the truck careened back across the street, Stinky hopping as fast as he could and trying hard to pull off his right boot which was still stuck. If the running board had been on the truck it would have saved him, but it had been gone since fat Leopold, his son in law, had stomped it off. In spite of the precarious state of his laces the boot would not come off. Ma was sitting there looking aggrieved. She had dropped her cigarette when Stinky had run up the curb. Just as the truck was about to crash into the curb on the east side of the street he caught the choke with his sleeve and the truck started hiccoughing along running very badly. It gave Stinky his chance. He lunged back into the truck and slammed home the clutch. The truck stopped and Stinky pushed the choke back in and the engine smoothed out to a soft purr. Stinky yanked his door shut, slipped the truck into first gear and slowly pulled out to start the rounds.

"Where's Jonas?" Ma was looking around. "I thought Jonas was comin'. Is he on your runnin' board?"

"Ain't got no runnin' board." Stinky craned his neck to look into the back of the truck. "I don't see him." He turned right at the corner, went around the block, and there was Jonas standing in the street in front of Stinky's house, holding the board. Stinky pulled up to the curb and Jonas deftly slipped the board in front of the rear wheel as Stinky stopped.

"What are you doin' boy? we got trash to pick uuuuuuhhhhhhhhp!" Stinky leapt out of the truck, letting out the clutch, which jerked the truck forward so hard Dora's head bounced off the back window of the cab.

Stinky began to dance around and holler in the street. "I'm bein' stung! I'm bein bit! Somethin's got me!" Stinky beat on his own back end trying to stop the stinging, all the time craning his neck and running in circles trying to see what it was.

Dora rubbed the back of her head and in doing so looked down at the truck seat. "Found my cigarette."

Stinky got his pants fire put out by sitting in the frost covered weeds along side the sidewalk, then went back to the truck. He climbed in, then he climbed right back out again. He inspected the seat suspiciously, glared at Dora, making sure she had her cigarette in her mouth, then climbed in again.

"Pull out the board boy." Jonas pulled the board out from under the wheel and the truck began coasting down the hill.

"Jump on boy! Jump on the truck!" Stinky was shouting out the window looking back at Jonas who was just standing there holding the board.

"Slow down Pa." Jonas slung the board over against the curb and began running after the truck. It was careening back and forth across the street with Stinky hanging out the window watching

Jonas's progress. Stinky had forgotten to put the truck in second gear so when he let out the clutch while still in first gear the right rear tire just skidded causing the truck to lurch around sideways. This gave Jonas his chance to grab on just as the truck lurched to a stop on the level at the corner.

"I'm on Pa. I made it. We can go." Jonas was sitting on the tailboard swinging his feet and hollering. "Pa? Pa, I'm on. Pa is the truck runnin'? It's arful quiet. Pa?"

"Push boy." Stinky was out of the truck shoving it out into the intersection. If he turned right here it was downhill to the mill. "Get down and push boy."

"Gee Pa it's easier if the truck's runnin' ain't it." Jonas mused watching Stinky's face turn red from exertion.

After a few joint shoves, the truck began to roll on it's own and Stinky jumped in, slammed the truck into second gear and let out on the clutch. The engine spun over but nothing happened. Then Stinky realized the key was turned off. Just as the truck was about to lurch to a stop Stinky got the key turned and the engine started with a tremendous backfire, which startled the workers at the mill, and Dora. He turned the truck back left and headed over to the dump, figuring since he was this close he would unload a little trash now. As he turned the corner, he looked back up the street only to see a familiar figure. It took him a whole block to work out that it was Jonas standing back there. Stinky swung the truck around in the drive of the bed spring factory, and headed back up the hill. Jonas was standing right where the truck had started.

"Gee Pa you runneded off and left me again. I thought you wanted me to come Pa." Jonas was genuinely hurt. "Do you think I'm a snake Pa so's you don't want me?"

"Get in the truck boy." After making sure Jonas was securely on the back of the truck, Stinky swung the truck around again and cruised to the dump to empty what was already in the truck.

Stinky often had trouble unloading at the dump. Ma found things she wanted almost as fast as he could shovel garbage out. Three legged chairs seemed to be her favorite. She found one almost every stop. Magazines with pictures and not too many words she liked too, if they hadn't gotten wet, or didn't have too much garbage stuck on them. Kitchen cabinets and iceboxes, hand mixers and kerosene lanterns, sad irons and old bicycles abounded. Stinky hauled things like that off to his old Pappy's barn that he shared with Morely Wofford. Once, He and Leopold had found a windmill and drug it off with the legs dangling over the back of the truck and the Air-Motor blades spinning in front of the cab. He should have taken the windmill out of gear so that pump rod didn't drag up and down across the top of the truck as the blades turned. It made a crease in the linoleum on the patched roof of the truck that caught water and leaked sometimes. Stinky had even drug off cars from the dump.

This morning, steam was rising from the trash as the sun came up and burnt off the frost. Stinky worked his way around to the west side of the biggest pile of garbage, carefully backed up till he hit the Morgan's old coal stove laying on it's side on the edge of the pile, then slipped the truck into neutral and left it idling.

Jonas had hopped out as Stinky began backing up, and was trekking out across the piles looking for good stuff. He found toys that were perfectly good all the time and took them out to his Pappy's barn, or gave them to the neighborhood kids. Pappy Randall had been dead for years, but it still seemed like his place. The house on the land had been sold to Morely Wofford, but the barn and outbuildings and a few acres was still theirs, and they were full to overflowing with trash that was too good to throw away. Often, Dora would go out to join Jonas in looking for good stuff. This morning Dora, like she often did, got a new cigarette going and climbed down out of the truck.

"Dora, don't be bringin' no three legged chairs today. We ain't got the room for them to home." Stinky said as he finished parking.

" I ain't lookin' for no chairs today." Dora answered, "There's good dishes out here all the time. Clean too." The ones with flowers or pictures on them were her favorites.

Stinky jumped out of the truck, pulled the old scoop shovel with the big hole worn through the bottom out of the gap between the bed and the truck cab, climbed into the back of the truck, and began shoveling out the trash. He worked in spurts and jerks conserving energy for the long day ahead and enjoying the view. Even the air smelled clean this morning, with the garbage still frozen and just beginning to thaw in the sun. The shoveling got easier toward the bottom of the truck. Most of what was in there was paper that had been wet and was plastered together and would come out in big wet chunks. Stinky could, now, actually see the truck bed in a place or two (the first time in months) and was thinking of quitting. He stepped back to observe his work and found himself squatting on one leg with the other leg dangling under the truck. The shoveling job had been too good. Stinky had shoveled out the only thing that was keeping the trash, and people, from falling through the holes in the bed. Stinky tried to pull his leg out by simply raising straight up on the leg still up in the truck, but he seemed to be stuck on something and couldn't pull up. He then decided to sit down and pull the leg up out of the hole while seated. He scrunched around and worked his left leg out from under him and out in front of him and sat down. The water in the trash still in the bottom of the truck began to seep through Stinky's pants (especially at the burn holes.) as Stinky began to yank and squirm trying to pull his right leg up. At that point, Stinky began to have a strange sensation in his right shin. It didn't feel right. It was kind of hot, and something smelled like it was burning.

"Jonas, Dora!! Help I'm burnin.'" Stinky began to work frantically at getting his leg loose. "Jonaaaassss? Dorrrrraaaaa!"

Jonas was reading a comic book. At least he was looking at the pictures. Reading was hard work. He often found comics in the dump and took them home. This one was about some guy that could fly and it looked like bullets from a Tommy gun just bounced right off him. Superman. Wow. The sound of shouting interrupted Jonas's perusing and he climbed up on the nearest pile to see what was going on. He couldn't see his Pa, but he could hear him.

"I'm on fire!" Stinky was getting downright excited. "Jonas! Dora!"

Jonas trotted toward the truck mystified by the shouting. When he reached the truck he could see his Pa's foot sticking out the bottom of the truck, his pant cuff hooked over the rusted out end of the muffler.

"Jonas! Dora! Help!" from his position, Stinky couldn't see Jonas standing there contemplating the leg sticking down from the truck.

"Pa? How'd you get under there Pa. What you doin' under the truck Pa?" Jonas got down on his hands and knees to study on it.

"Get me loose boy. I'm a burnin' my ankle off."

"Should I turn off the truck Pa? The truck is burnin' you." Jonas was peeking through the slats on the truck.

"Yeah. No! Just unhook my pants boy." Stinky figured the battery might not be charged up enough to start the truck again yet.

Jonas clambered up into the truck and much to Stinky's surprise, began trying to untie his clothesline belt.

"What in tarnation are you doin' Boy" Stinky was beginning to think his pants would soon burst into flames like the rags in the stove had done. "Get down below and get my britches loose from whatever they is catched on!" Stinky's voice rose in pitch and volume, as his shin got hotter and hotter.

Jonas hopped back out of the truck, got down on his hands and knees, crawled under the truck and pulled the cuff of Stinky's pants loose from the rusty tail pipe. Stinky's foot shot up through the hole and Stinky fairly flew out of the truck, ran over to an old truck tire that was standing on edge with ice topped rainwater in it, and stuck his foot into the water. Then he sloshed the water all over his shin trying to cool it down.

"You'll get your boot full o' water Pa." Jonas looked shocked at what Stinky was doing. "You always tell me that when I step in a puddle Pa."

"Get in the truck boy."

Dora was clambering back over the piles towing what looked to be the signs from one of the markets in town. The market had changed owners and the new proprietor had taken down the big tin signs for Coca Cola, Nehi, Cooper Tires, Folgers Coffee and Holsum Bread that had previously adorned the side of the building. "Patch the barn up a bit." She said, and stood them up on edge along the side of the truck bed with some help from Jonas.

"You got your boot full o' water Elroy." Dora had noticed that with each of Stinky's steps, water squirted out a hole in the side of his boot.

"Get in the truck Dora" Stinky slid the truck into low and pulled out of the dump, the bald tires on the right side spinning in the mud as they went.

Stinky had worked up some appetite shoveling. "Hey Dora did we have doughnuts yesterday?"

Dora thought hard. "What flavor?"

"It don't matter what flavor. I just wanna know if we et 'em yesterday."

Dora thought some more, "I wasn't with you yesterday."

Stinky got the truck into third gear then hollered out the window to Jonas. "Hey boy! Did we have doughnuts yesterday?"

"What flavor?" Jonas hollered back.

"It don't matter what flavor. I just wanna know if we et 'em yesterday."

" Do snakeses eat doughnuts? Was we supposed to? " Jonas was feeling abused, "I hate missin' things."

"It don't matter if we was supposed to or not. I want to know if we had doughnuts yesterday?"

"I disremember Pa. Were the doughnuts good Pa? I hate missing out."

"I don't know boy. Well what day is it today?" Maybe Stinky could remember what days the L&M offered fresh doughnuts and pastries for breakfast.

"Tuesday" Dora answered after a short deliberation.

"Thursday" Jonas answered.

Stinky thought it out carefully. "Friday. Today is payday. It's Friday."

"Where was I Thursday Pa? I hate missing out. " Jonas had climbed down the slats on the side of the truck and was standing on the right hand running board leaning in the window so he could hear better.

"I don't know boy. You wasn't with me. Your brother Martin was with me yesterday."

"Did I miss doughnuts Pa? I hate missing things."

"I disremember boy, but I think the L&M bakes on Friday mornin' cause we have doughnuts on payday."

"Elroy I want me some doughnuts" Dora was thinking back to the last time they had gotten doughnuts at the L&M. "I like them doughnuts."

Stinky cruised up main and up to the square. He turned down the street beside the L&M where he parked the truck. He decided the battery might be charged up enough to start the truck now and shut the truck off.

"Go see if there's any doughnuts boy." Stinky relaxed in the truck. Jonas hopped down from the truck and trotted down the narrow alley between the L&M and the barbershop.

Enos Mack, head cook at L&M Restaurant, had been fussing with his wife Veda. They had fought or drank all night, or at least until Enos went in to work at four thirty AM to do the pastry baking at the L&M. He had been a little distracted, and a lot drunk, that morning. The doughnut batter had wound up with a whole one-pound sack of salt in it. Grunt Andress, the first customer of the morning, found out. The whole batch had been thrown out, and Enos had started the morning baking over from scratch.

Two-day-old doughnuts were thrown out on the mornings when new doughnuts were made. Stinky had seen as many as four donuts in the trash, and to Stinky's mind, they were as good as new if you had coffee to dunk them in. The food trash was picked up by Morris Drum to feed to his pigs, but he only came around every few days and then always in the afternoon. Jonas opened the big wooden lid to the garbage bin and right on top were two big brown paper grocery sacks with greasy spots on the outside. Jonas looked inside one. It was full of big wonderful smelling glazed doughnuts. Then Jonas looked in the other sack. It was full of maple bars and chocolate coated doughnuts. It was a lifetime worth of doughnuts. It was unbelievable. Jonas just stared.

"Hey boy. is there doughnuts?" Stinky's voice rang down the alley.

"Yeah Pa they's doughnuts." Jonas still stared.

"Bring us some boy." Stinky shouted again, then as an aside to Dora, "Probably eatin' all the good ones."

Jonas grabbed up a sack and ran toward the truck looking behind in case someone discovered their mistake and came out to get them back. He ran across the street to the truck, carefully set the sack down in the back of the truck, then ran back for more.

"Where you goin' boy? Ain't there any doughnuts?" The grocery sack didn't translate into doughnuts to Stinky.

"They's hunnerts Pa. Hunnerts! You won't think I'm a snake after this Pa. Snakeses don't get hunnerts o' doughnuts." Jonas was running back to the trash bin. He looked somewhat fearfully at the back door of the L&M afraid someone would come out and take his doughnuts away as he grabbed up the other sack and ran back for the truck.

Stinky had gotten out of the truck and gone around to look at what Jonas had put in the back. He was almost as astounded as Jonas when he saw the big sack full of doughnuts. "Them don't look like no two day old doughnuts to me."

"Gimme a doughnut Elroy." Dora was scrounging around in her purse pouring the scraps of tobacco from the bottom into a cigarette paper. Surprisingly most of what was in the bottom of her purse was in fact tobacco. "Don't hog 'em Elroy. Gimme one."

Jonas came running out of the Alley carrying the other sack full of the fancy doughnuts. "Pa. Pa! Ain't it somethin' Pa? Sacks o' hunnerts o' doughnuts."

"Where'd you get these boy?" Stinky was eyeing Jonas suspiciously.

"In the same place you showed me Pa. Right under the wooden lid where the other scraps is. Right where you showed me. Is I a snake now Pa?"

"Could be boy. You just take those right back where you got em." Stinky knew he had taught that boy better. "I'll bring this sack and check on this."

Jonas looked hurt. "I ain't a snake Pa. Really I ain't. I looked and I don't look like no snakes I ever seed. A snake ain't got legs or feet or eyebrows or nothin' like I got."

"Show me where you got these here doughnuts boy." Stinky started up the alley with Jonas following along.

"It was right where you told me to look." Jonas was slinking along behind Stinky "I really ain't no snake Pa."

"Show me boy."

"It's right cheer Pa." Jonas lifted the lid to the scrap box. "They was right on top. I ain't no snake Pa. A ox maybe, but no snake. A ox don't lie do they Pa. Only snakeses lieses"

86

"Let's ask inside if they was s'posed to throw them doughnuts out."

"But Pa. They might think we stealded um." Jonas was nervous at the thought. "I never stealded um Pa."

"Knock on the door of the kitchen boy." Stinky's mouth was watering at the smell of the sacks full of doughnuts and wondering if they would miss just one even if they was accidentally thrown out and they wanted them back. He figured he better not eat one though on account of bein' a good example to the boy.

Jonas knocked on the door timidly. "I knocked Pa. They didn't answer. We can go Pa."

"Now hold on boy. You knock on that door good and loud. We gots to ask about these here doughnuts." Stinky was trying to sneak one out of the sack and into his pocket without Jonas seeing.

"What you want Stinky?" Enos looked balefully out of the screen door at Jonas and Stinky. The night was catching up on him, and he had run out of booze in his stash in the L&M stockroom.

"Need to know if you want these here doughnuts Mr. Mack." Stinky held his hat in his hand while he talked to a big important man like Enos Mack, the morning cook at the L&M. He had to be important for all those rich folks to come eat his cooking.

"They was in the garbage wasn't they?" Enos considered his reply carefully. "You can have anything that's in the garbage, if you judge you want it."

"Thank you Mr. Mack. Much 'bliged." Stinky watched Enos go back in the kitchen slamming the door behind him. "You ought to be an important man like Mr. Mack someday, boy."

"I told you I wasn't no snake Pa. Only snakeses would take stuff weren't theirn." Jonas was hugging the sack of doughnuts to himself smelling the sweet smell and feeling the warmth.

"Let's go to the truck boy." Stinky was staring down into the open sack trying to decide. Jonas joined in looking in Stinky's brown paper sack.

"What you reckon those long bars got on top o' them Pa."

"Maple icing."

"Icing from Maple street?"

"Maple trees." Stinky was still deciding which one he wanted as they stepped out into the street.

Jonas was contemplating a doughnut with icing being made from a tree. "I don't reckon I would like icing made of a tree. Maybe it'd taste like akerns. I et akerns oncet. They was poor eatin, even when you is hungry, and them akerns sat right poorly on my stomach. Think maybe I want one o' them normal round sticky donuts." Jonas was overwhelmed by the majesty of the decision he was being allowed to make. "Glazed." Jonas had decided.

"Glazed?"

"Glazed!" Stinky had decided too.

They had both stopped in the middle of the street and were staring down into Stinky's brown paper sack which he had set down in the street.

Hooooonnnnnnnnkkkkkkkkkkk. Homer Lane had a bad temper and a long memory, and no love for Stinky or his family. He was tardy on paying for his trash pickup nearly every month, and Stinky passed by Homer's house about every other time because his house was on the "collection due" paper Marvin McDonald wrote up every week. Homer drove the big semi truck that traveled between the small town lumberyards and the supply house up east. And today he was running late, and on a mission to make up time.

Jonas dropped his sack and jumped for the curb. Stinky grabbed his sack by the corner and ran for his truck. The sack burst open spewing doughnuts across the street. The truck passed in front of Jonas and behind Stinky flattening Jonas's sack with the left front wheel and running over all but one of Stinky's with the right front the dual rears and then the tandem trailer wheels.

One, lone, untouched maple bar lay in the street.

"Pa he smushed the doughnuts. Look at that Pa." Jonas stood looking at the sacks not contemplating the loss, but the awful power of a big truck. "Wow Pa. That was somethin'."

"Get in the truck boy." Stinky picked up the one remaining maple-bar and looked at it ruefully, then at the mess in the street. "Here's you a doughnut Dora."

"Thought you had lots o doughnuts Elroy. Where'd you put all them doughnuts?" Dora was picking some gravel out of the bottom of her maple bar.

"Eat your doughnut Dora." Stinky was still wondering if he scraped some of the stuff in the sack up, if there would still be something good to eat, just sort of already chewed.

Dora bit into the maple bar smearing the sticky icing on her face in the process. "Salty."

Stinky, unsure whether Dora approved of the maple bar or not after that comment, climbed into the truck, turned on the key, and stepped on the starter pedal. A fain't groan, then a rattle came out of the starter. He stepped on the starter pedal again, and this time, just a groan, not even a rattle.

"Get out and push boy." Stinky climbed out of the truck eyeing the best way to go. First back up the truck, to get around a sedan now parked in front of them, and then west from the square and down the little incline toward the Memorial Hall. Stinky went around in front of the truck and began to push backwards. Jonas climbed down out of the bed of the truck and began pushing forward. Stinky was stronger but Jonas had gravity on his side. The truck began to roll forward.

Stinky tried to jump clear but the burnt hole in his pant leg caught over the big tow-hook welded to the front bumper bracket and held him fast. Jonas felt the truck move and gave a mighty heave. Just enough to push the truck over a rough spot in the street and pinch Stinky between the truck and the forty-six Mercury parked in front of the truck.

"Dora, step on the brake. Hold the truck. It's a mashin' my leg." Stinky got one foot up on the bumper of the Mercury but the other was held fast.

"Pa the truck ain't movin' and I cain't budge her." Jonas was shouting from in back o' the truck. "I'm tryin Pa. She ain't movin". It's easier when she runs Pa.

"Come over here boy."

Jonas came around the truck and looked at his father. "Why there is a car parked in front of the truck Pa." He was genuinely surprised. "Think we ought to steer the truck around the car Pa? "

"Help me push boy."

"I was pushin' Pa. It ain't no use. I can't hardly push just the truck and I ain't never gonna be able to push the truck and that there car." Jonas was studying the problem carefully. "Can you come round and help me Pa?"

" Let's push the other way boy." Stinky's leg was beginning to tingle like a foot gone to sleep. "Come help boy."

"Oh. Oh! backerds! OK Pa." Jonas stepped in next of Stinky to push. They strained together using the Mercury to push off of. "It's hard Pa. Like I said I can't budge her."

Stinky looked at the truck in bewilderment. It shouldn't be this hard to get to move. Maybe he was just weak. He was hungry. "Push again boy."

They both pushed, muscles straining, but to no avail.

"Can I take my foot off'n the brake Elroy? It makes my leg tarred." Dora was scrunched down in the seat sideways holding on the brake with her left foot.

"Let off the break Dora! Let's try it again boy."

"OK Pa but it's hard. Mighty hard." Jonas looked doubtfully at the truck. He prepared himself and then gave a mighty heave. The truck rolled backwards easily over the little hump where it was parked and then about five feet further dragging Stinky with it by his pant leg. When it had gone as far back as it would from the one heave it started back forward knocking Stinky down and dragging him along by the pant leg. Jonas leapt out of the way just before the truck ran back into the Mercury.

"Whered' you go Pa." Jonas was looking around "Pa?"

Stinky was lying under the truck. The radiator and the front axle just cleared his chest but both rubbed off a considerable amount of grease and oil on the way over him. Stinky looked up under the hood and was surprised to see loose wires on the starter. He wiggled them around a bit, tightened the battery cable on the starter with his fingers then laboriously drug himself out from under the truck on the left side. Jonas had walked around the truck looking for him and was on the right side of the truck. Stinky climbed in the truck, turned on the key and stepped on the starter pedal. The truck spun over smoothly, started, and idled along. Stinky slid the truck into reverse, backed up a few feet and pulled out of the parking spot. He turned left a couple of blocks down, at Garrison, to go south, down to the start of his route.

"Where's Jonas? I thought Jonas was a goin with us." Dora was looking around like she expected him to pop up out of the floor of the truck.

"Isn't he in the back?" Stinky craned his neck around to see. No Jonas.

Stinky turned the truck back east at the big Carnegie Library then turned back north at the next street. He turned right on fourth and stopped across the street from where they had just been parked.

Jonas was sitting on the curb sulking."Gee Pa. The truck started. You run off without me again Pa. I ain't a snake Pa. Honest. You want me along Pa? I'm better help than any snake Pa."

"Get in the truck boy."

The Standard Station was just a few blocks away and Stinky, remembering the low tire, drove south, up the hill and turned into the station, next to the island, where the air hose was always neatly hung. The bell rang as Stinky's truck passed over the rubber hose and Ernie Sharp jumped up from his chair and quickly stepped to the door. His progress slowed when he saw who it was. Stinky had been in just a couple of days before and Ernie figured Stinky was just after air for that inner, rear, tire that always leaked.

"Howdy Ernie!" Stinky hung out the window of his truck to talk, "Reckon I need some air in that right rear, inner tire. She done got low on me again."

"Stinky, you know I ain't sposed to give you air lessen you buy gasoline." Ernie good naturedly ribbed Stinky as he began to uncoil the hose, "Standard Oil would go broke if we done that for everyone."

"Now Ernie, you knowed I boughted gasoline on Tuesday, and I don't need no more today." Stinky answered defending his request; "I never got no air Tuesday."

"Well, I reckon, just this once won't bankrupt Mr. Rocketfeller." Ernie answered as he finished uncoiling the hose. "How many pounds you want in her Stinky?"

"She says sixty, but I reckon at her age that might be a bit much." Stinky considered the problem, "Maybe forty?"

"Forty it is then Stinky" Ernie answered, grateful that Stinky didn't ask him to risk his life putting sixty pounds of pressure in the old cracked tire. Carefully pushing the long air chuck into the hole in the outer wheel and onto the long valve sticking out of the inside wheel, Ernie watched the gauge built into his air chuck. He was proud of that chuck, only one like it in town. None of that putting the air in, then checking with a pencil gauge, and then more air, or less. He could do a perfect job every time with just one tool. "There you go Stinky. Forty!"

"Much 'bliged Earnie." Stinky pushed the truck into gear, "I'll buy me some gas next Tuesday!"

Stinky slowly drove up and around the square, then south on Main down to Chestnut, where he turned back west and across Garrison, down to West Chestnut where he started his route on Fridays. It looked like he was in the right part of town since there was trash put out at the curb. That was a good sign. Stinky still wasn't completely accustomed to the trashcans being pulled out to the street for him. For years he had been walking around to back yards to get the trash, and putting the cans back in their place. He missed seeing the back yards, but not fighting the dogs, or wading through snow or mud.

"There's trash Elroy." Dora surprised him with her astute observations. "You drove past it."

"We start at the other end of the street Dora."

"Hey Pa! There's trash." Jonas was hanging over the slats on the side of the truck hollering down toward Stinky's window. "You droveded past it."

"We start at the other end of the street." Stinky shouted out the half open window.

"I heard the first time Elroy." Dora was working on another cigarette made from the stubs of cigarettes found in the ashtray of the truck. "You don't need to shout at me Elroy Randall."

Stinky refrained from answering, recognizing that it was futile.

The number three Randall son, Arthur (short for MacArthur, which everyone had forgotten within a week of his birth), had driven the truck for Stinky the day before. It was Arthur's day off from his regular job at the Hercules dynamite plant. He was high class, and smoked Camels by the pack, stubbing them out in the big ashtray up on the dash, and leaving the butts there. Dora could get nearly a half-day's worth of roll-your-owns out of his leftovers after the days that Arthur drove for Stinky.

Stinky reached the end of Chestnut and crossed over Baker blvd into the cemetery. Stinky considered that "blvd" every time he crossed Baker and wondered how in the world you were supposed to pronounce that. The cemetery was arrayed on the eastern face of a hill that paralleled the street. Stinky always thought it would be a lovely place to watch for the second coming, the top of that hill in Park Cemetery. Maybe he could buy himself and Dora a little plot there someday. He cruised up the hill and slowed at the top to turn right to the cemetery owner's house and Park Cemetery Monument

Shop. This was his first Friday stop. The sun was up, the sky was blue, and Stinky's stomach was growling. It was always hard work these first few stops. Being hungry didn't help.

"I can't lift it Pa." Jonas was straining at the fifty-gallon-drum of trash near the back of the truck. "There's somethin' in it Pa."

Stinky climbed out of the truck and began to rummage around in the can. He shoveled a good deal of the trash out of the can and into the truck by hand with Jonas helping by picking up what fell on the ground and throwing it back in the can.

"Now let's try it boy."

Stinky had unloaded maybe ten pounds worth of trash but the can still weighed in at about what he and Jonas weighed together. Stinky nearly stood on his head trying to get the last of the trash out of the can and see what was making it so heavy. His feet were up in the air flailing around, but when he was that far down, he blocked out most of the light, so he couldn't see well. So he pulled out all the trash he could grab and flung it in the truck.

"I'll dive in there again, then we can go." Stinky clambered head first into the can to get the last of the trash out of the bottom. Jonas misunderstood and leaned down to lift, not paying attention to what Stinky was doing. Jonas gave one mighty heave and the can tipped toward Stinky, and Jonas misinterpreting what was happening gave another mighty effort and turned the can over on its side.

Stinky flopped over with the can, knocking his head on both sides of it as he went. Jonas, being surprised by the can falling over, fell down against the can and started it on it's trip east, down the hill, through the cemetery.

The Gravely brothers who ran the monument shop had been watching to see what Stinky would do with the trash-can. They had gathered at the big garage door of the shop to watch. Earlier that morning, they had taken a big piece of a broken headstone and had put it in the bottom of the fifty-gallon drum as a joke.

On the first revolution of the can, the headstone piece flopped up on Stinky's chest, wedging him in the can. The weight of the stone forced air in and out of his lungs as the barrel rotated. With every revolution the air whistled out of Stinky's lungs with a shriek. After about ten revolutions, the can, having picked up a moderate amount of momentum, crashed into a six-inch tall grey limestone wall that surrounded one family's plot and careened into a clear walkway between the graves.

"Elroy you dropped the can down the hill" Dora, who was still sitting in the truck, had finally got her cigarette going after a miscue with rolling a filter up in her roll-your-own by accident, was watching in the mirror as the can crashed down the hill.

Jonas was picking chat out of this hand from falling down, and hadn't noticed the can was

still rolling or that Stinky was trapped inside.

"AAAAAAAAAAAAAAAAAAAAAAEEEEEEEEEEEEEEEEEEEEEEEE" came from the can steamrolling down the hill. It echoed eerily, scaring Jonas nearly out of his wits. He climbed in the truck cab forcing his Ma to scoot over. Dora took this to mean Stinky was ready to go and slid on over into the drivers seat.

She started up the truck and drove around the circle drive of the monument shop, waving to the Gravely boys as she went by.

"AAAAAAAAAAAAAAAAAAAAAAAAAAA umph!" The rolling can crept off the path and plowed into a small grave-stone, jumped another small grave hummock, passed an access road and was sent a little more south by another limestone wall surrounding another family plot. This time Stinky's legs bounced off the low wall and brought tears to his eyes and temporarily curtailed his shouting.

Dora maneuvered the truck around the drive and accelerated down the hill a plume of blue smoke obscuring the back of the truck. She was assuming Stinky was riding the tailgate and they were going after the runaway can. Jonas was quivering in the seat, but Dora just figured the boy was cold. Dora charged after the errant can, saw it turn toward the road, and there was her chance. She shifted into second gear to try to intersect the can's path but it jumped the corner block and crashed out in front of the truck instead of hitting the side of the truck like Dora had planned. She plowed into the can bending it just enough to make it roll poorly. It also dislodged the stone from on top of Stinky and spat him out of the can and onto the edge of the roadway. The truck wheels just missed him as he rolled to the right. Dora though was still in pursuit of the can. When it caught on a headstone and stopped just a few feet down the road and Dora pumped hard on the brake pedal and skidded to a stop.

"We caught it Elroy." Ma was trying to light her cigarette again. She had knocked off the fire end of it when she hit the can. "Help your Pa with the can boy."

Jonas climbed out of the truck fearfully looking around for the demon that had made that awful sound. Stinky came up from behind the truck, limping and groaning at the effort. "There's why she was so heavy Pa. There was a rock in the can. See it Pa. A big rock in the trash. We don't take rockses do we Pa? It's a big heavy rock Pa."

"Put the can in the truck boy. We don't haul no rocks." Stinky climbed in the passenger side of the truck, groaning and moaning, his wheezing causing Dora to look sideways at him.

"We ain't so young anymore is we Elroy." Ma was enjoying her cigarette even though the paper burnt too fast and dropped burning tobacco down her front.

Jonas carried the can around to the back of the truck worrying some about the bent can and about leaving that rock. He tossed the can up into the truck and Dora took off back up to the monument shop.

"Unload the can." Stinky shouted out the window. Nothing happened. "Unload the can!"

"I heared you the first time Elroy. I don't lift no cans, and you should know that by now." Ma continued to sit, contentedly puffing away. "I ain't lifted no cans since I had Jonas and it busted something in my belly."

"I ain't talking to you Dora." Stinky climbed out to see what had happened to Jonas, and why he didn't unload the can. Jonas wasn't in the truck. Stinky unloaded the can and then looked east down the hill. There was a familiar figure standing down the hill. Stinky climbed back in the truck and Dora eased the truck back down the hill.

"Why Elroy! There's Jonas!" Ma stopped the truck with a jerk.

"You run off and left me Pa. Don't you want me to come along Pa? I loaded the can in the truck Pa. Ain't I good help Pa? I ain't no snake Pa. Honest."

"Get in the truck boy." Stinky's stomach growled as he absentmindedly rubbed his burnt shin, thinking that maybe, they were going to run late all day.

First stop across Baker blvd was the other monument shop in town, owned and run by Norman Hook Jr. and his son Norman Hook the third. The shop had been started shortly after the war-between-the-states, by Norman Hook (the first). He had been a southern sympathizer. He had worked up at the Park Cemetery monument shop at the end of the "War of Northern Aggression" and had refused to cut stones for Union soldiers. He was invited to leave Park Cemetery's employ. It wasn't that the folks at Park Cemetery were strictly Union backers, they happily took money from both sides. Dead was dead and money was money they figured. Norman (the first) found some investors, local businessmen (some of the same ones suspected of helping Quantril's Raiders during the war) and set up shop just outside the main gate of Park Cemetery. Stinky's grandpap had sold moonshine to north and south equally, so Stinky picked up trash at both places. Sometimes there was good stuff in the trash at Norman's place, so he always dug through it carefully. He had gotten dull and broken stone cutting tools several times. Monty would give him a dime each for chipped or mushroomed chisels. When Stinky had first brought them to

Monty he said, "Them's great steel for making knives." So Stinky always looked for steel in the trash. Sadly, nothing good today. Just last year's calendar and bean cans from the Hook's lunches at the shop.

Stinky and Jonas worked along steadily; lifting and dumping cans into the back of the truck as Dora swerved back and forth across Chestnut. When they stopped at Slates' Store at the corner of Center and Chestnut to pick up the trash, Stinky reached in and shut off the truck. "I gotta stop. My stomach won't give me no peace." Jonas pulled the big trash can out to the street and Stinky was disappointed not to find any packaged goods of any kind in the trash. Not even any two or three day old bread.

"I'm goin' in the store." Stinky rubbed his chest where the piece of monument stone had bruised it, as he walked up to the entrance of the store. The door sat on an angle to Center and Chestnut streets under a shallow porch. Stinky stopped at the door, took off his furry cap and smoothed back his hair, then pushed open the door, the cowbell hooked on a rope on the door, announcing his arrival.

Omer Slates was in the storeroom to the back of the store when Stinky came in. Omer hurried out at the tinkle of the bell. His smile faded some when he saw who it was but he still spoke in his normal courteous tone. "What can I help you with Sti........ uh. Mr. Randall?"

"Kinder Hungary. Got any old stuff. Bread or such?" Stinky never asked for handouts. "I'll trade for pickin' up your trash."

"I ain't got any out-'o-date stuff today St....uh...Mr. Randall." Omer was struggling to remember Stinky's given name.

"Could I trade you trash pickup for a few items?"

"Let me look at my books Stin...uhh Elroy." Omer finally hit on Stinky's name. He pulled out the big black ledger from under the counter that ran from end to end on the north side of the store. He quickly looked up "Stinky", couldn't find a record, then remembered and looked under "Randall". "Uhh well now Elroy, it seems you traded this weeks trash pickup for a ceegar, a Grapette and some roasted peanuts."

"I'll trade you next weeks trash for a Grapette, some roasted peanuts, and a crackerjack." Stinky was figuring in his head but his stomach was interfering. "I don't need no ceegar this week. I ain't had no more new grandkids."

Omer was gratified to hear that, "Well that sounds fair enough." Omer pulled out a small paper sack and the silver peanut-scoop and got a few peanuts out of the barrel. He weighed them carefully on the big white counter scale, reading the price per pound figures until it reached what he thought was fair value for the trash pickup. The first time Stinky had proposed this type of trade, Omer had called the city offices to ask about it. They had referred him to Melvin McDonald. Melvin had assured him that the deal was legitimate and had asked Omer to always give Stinky a fair deal and to keep the receipts. Melvin squared it all up monthly when he collected the trash payments. The peanuts were still warm after being taken out of the big barrel roaster out back. "Here's your peanuts and the box of Crackerjacks." Omer wrote out a receipt and Stinky put his mark on it.

"Much 'bliged." Stinky opened the Coke case and pulled out a bottle of Grapette. "I'll return the bottle."

Omer had, as was his custom, been carefully taking note of everywhere Stinky had touched. Stinky opened the Grapette on the opener on the front of the Coke case and headed out the door. Omer pulled out the brown glass bottle of Lysol and a clean cloth from under the counter, and went out carefully wiping down the handle to the pop case, the doorknob and everything else Stinky might have touched. He waved the Lysol soaked rag in the air hoping to kill whatever that was he was smelling, then carefully noted the trade in his ledger. Omer was thinking that Stinky looked rougher than usual. Kind of disheveled.

Stinky walked back down the sidewalk munching on the first of the peanuts as he went, climbed in the cab of the truck, and Dora cruised across the road to the next trash pile.

"This one ain't good Dora. They ain't paid this month." Stinky had to watch Dora or she would pick up trash that wasn't theirs. "Go to the next one."

Stinky munched contentedly on the peanuts, drinking the Grapette, feeling the food settle his stomach, as Dora started the truck. She pushed the shifter into first and then let out the clutch a little too quickly just as Stinky was getting a swallow. Stinky bounced the bottle off his false teeth knocking the upper out of his mouth and into his lap. The teeth gave him trouble when he was eating anything solid. The upper plate didn't fit quite right. Stinky had found the teeth in Elisha Slaught's trash when the Slaught family cleaned out the house after the old man died. Stinky had broken off one corner of the top plate so his one tooth on the top-back would clear and wore them ever since. Stinky pulled the bottom plate out of his mouth and stuck both the top and bottoms in his shirt-pocket and went on munching contentedly. He just had that one tooth to chew with. It was the only one that really worked anyway.

About every house had trash on the curb. Hardware store trashcans, fifty gallon drums, cardboard boxes, dainty floral-decorated bath and kitchen tins, milk baskets and wooden crates, Stinky carefully emptied them all. Whether Stinky picked up everyone's trash was a mystery to everyone but Stinky and Melvin McDonald. Stinky always remembered who had paid. It was Melvin McDonald who "owned" the trash pick-up contract and collected the money monthly. The city collected a small percentage of the charges subcontracted out to Melvin. In return, Melvin's trash collectors could put the trash in the city dump. Melvin hired in folks, like the Randalls, to do the actual work. Melvin made money on it. The Randalls got paid for doing it, plus got the salvage rights, the city got the landfill fee and the trash got hauled every week. Everyone was happy. If Melvin had anyone who didn't pay he went around and talked to Stinky (or the other regular collector, Shep Holmes) and the trash was not picked up at that house. Melvin always had the trash picked up at his house and he never paid.

Mrs. Courtney, over on Centennial, tried putting her trash out with her neighbors for a while, exclaiming when Melvin caught on that "We don't have half the trash some of these folks do so why shouldn't we share trash pickup." Melvin wasn't impressed.

Besides Mrs. Courtney never split the cost with her neighbor. Stinky, though, would often pick up Mrs. Courtney's trash in trade for something she had saved back for him. Sometimes (like when he got the coat that Jonas wore all the time) it was a good deal, sometimes she tried to palm off something like a kerosene iron that had been on fire. She tried it out about once a year. Stinky never bit on the iron. Dora wouldn't use it even if Stinky could make it work. What in heaven's name did Dora have that needed ironed?

"Pa? I cain't lift this 'en" Jonas was standing looking down at an anvil. A big anvil.

Stinky was across the street picking up a paper grocery sack of garbage. "What is it?"

"A piece o' iron Pa." Jonas was measuring with his hands about twenty-four inches across to show Stinky "Bout this big."

Stinky tossed his trash in the truck and walked around to see what it was. " Anvil. Somebody throwed it out." Stinky squatted down to test the weight of the anvil and found it beyond his strength. "Help me boy."

Jonas leaned down and tugged on the anvil in concert with Stinky and it barely moved.

"One more time boy." Stinky and Jonas put their backs into it and scooted it just far enough to get the edge off the sidewalk. It began to tip and then, the side nearest Stinky sinking in the soft ground, fell over landing solidly on top of the toes of Stinky's boots. It was a good thing he was wearing boots about four sizes too large.

He had found the boots in Elsie Grundy's trash after she divorced her husband Farley. Farley was a big, tall, man with very large feet. Elsie knew the oversized boots were special made to fit Farley, so when she found them in the garage, she threw them out the big garage door, one landing on the trash pile and one in the gutter. Stinky had needed boots and saw them as a blessing, sitting down on the curb and lacing them on right then.

Stinky didn't even notice his toes were hooked until he tried to step back. He was seated immediately on the edge of the curb, his knees up and the toes of his boots trapped beneath the anvil, the wet of the ground soaking the seat of his pants, again.

"Help me get it off my toes boy."

"Do it hurt Pa? Your toes must be flat Pa. Oh Pa it looks like it 'ud pain ya arful Pa." Jonas was tugging at the anvil. "I cant' move it Pa."

"What you doin' Elroy?" Dora had smoked up the last of her cigarettes made from the remains in the ashtray already. "You gonna be long Elroy?" Dora climbed out of the truck and went around to the back. Old Mr Treadwell smoked and they had just picked up his trash. She began to rummage around in the sacks, looking for butts with no filters that she could get tobacco out of.

"I cain't do 'er Pa." Jonas passed a loud poot with the effort.

Stinky held out his hand to Jonas, "Help me stand up and I'll help you lift the thing of'n my boots."

Jonas pulled up Stinky and they both leaned over to tug on the anvil. Their heads met right at the bottom of the lean, making a loud thunk and causing both of them to set down abruptly.

Now both of them had wet seats and Jonas was softly blubbering "You din't haf to thump me Pa. I wuz tryin' Pa. I wuz. I ain't no snake Pa. Honest." Jonas hadn't noticed that Stinky was down too. "You hurt my head Pa."

"Help me up boy" Stinky was trying to stand up again.

"You lost your hat Pa." Jonas was retrieving Stinky's hat. "What knocked your hat off Pa?"

Stinky was putting his hat back on. "Help me up boy."

"Don't whack my head Pa." Jonas warily helped Stinky up.

"Help me lift boy." Stinky started to lean over then raised back up to avoid Jonas then began to lean down. Jonas being suspicious reared back up as soon as he was leaned over and whacked Stinky in the face with the back of his head and they both sat down again. Stinky's nose began to trickle blood and he pulled out his rag and held it on his nose. Jonas began to whimper again.

"Get in the truck boy." Stinky was unlacing his boots.

"Why'd you clunk me Pa. I ain't no snake Pa. Whats'a matter with your nose Pa.?" Jonas was standing back and eying Stinky. "Did you whack me with your nose Pa?"

Stinky pulled his feet out of his boots. One of his socks came off in the boot and he pulled it out and carried it over to the truck. He climbed into the cab and pulled his sock on. "Let's go on Dora. Get in the truck boy!"

Dora was still rummaging around in the back gathering up cigarette butts and stripping them and dumping the tobacco into the old Prince Albert can. "Just a minute Elroy." Now she was looking for some good paper to use. She had used up all the papers she had made from the German math book. Maybe there was something in her purse. Dora went around to the driver's seat and clambered up.

"You forgot your boots Pa. Don't you want your boots Pa?" Jonas was ineffectually tugging at Stinky's boots. "You want the Anvil Pa? This anvil don't look woreded out to me Pa. How do you know if a anvil is woreded out Pa? Is your boots woreded out Pa? Shouldn't we put them in the back o' the truck Pa? Ain't we s'posed to pick up all the trash at our houses Pa? Marvin won't like us leavin' stuff Pa."

"Get in the truck boy." Stinky was pulling on his sock and folding the hole in the end over and sticking it in between his big toe and the second toe. "Let's go home Ma."

"You forgot your boots Elroy." Ma was looking out the window studying the gutter to see if there was any paper there to make cigarettes out of. "You think grocery sack paper would make me a cigarette Elroy?"

"Let's go home Dora." Stinky looked balefully out at the trash up the street. "We're gonna run late all day."

"Is it lunch Elroy? I ain't very hungry yet." Dora was craning her neck around trying to see the courthouse clock while driving up Chestnut. "'course I had me that big funny looking donut."

"Maple bar." Stinky said his nose throbbing.

"Yeah, I had me that maple bar." Dora licked her lips remembering. "I think Mr. Mack should put less salt in 'em though."

She came up on the stoplight at Garrison, saw it turn yellow, forgot to pump the brakes at first, and then panicked and jammed down the brake pedal hard, without pushing in the clutch, which killed the engine and lurched the truck to a stop. Stinky caught unawares, hit himself in the eye with his Grapette bottle then lurched forward hitting his nose on the dash, starting it bleeding again.

Dora never noticed Stinky's discomfort, but busied herself searching under the seat for paper suitable for a cigarette, completely ignoring the traffic lights.

"De lide id dreen Dora." Stinky was holding the rag on his nose again. "We dan doe Dora."

Dora quit digging under the seat and raised up. She pushed on the starter pedal and nothing happened. "The truck won't start Elroy."

"Dry id adin Dora" Stinky blew his nose on his underwear hanky, trying to clear the clotted blood out.

"The truck won't go Elroy." Dora was just sitting there thinking about a cigarette.

Stinky climbed out of the truck, unwired, and opened the right side of the hood. He couldn't reach the battery cable on the starter from up top, so he crawled under the truck to pull on the battery cable like he had earlier. He reached up and twisted on the nut to the battery cable and he discovered Dora still had her foot on the pedal with the truck in gear and much to his surprise the truck started and lurched out into the street dragging Stinky with it. The light had turned red during the interval and a large bread van had begun to pull out just as Stinky's truck lurched out into the intersection. The bread truck bumper passed over Stinky's legs and crashed into his truck trapping him beneath both vehicles without touching him. The bread truck's huge front bumper deformed the fender, running board and door of Stinky's truck and pushed the whole truck sideways several yards.

The driver of the bread truck, Lew Maxwell, had been running late and was running the truck hard. It was overheating and spewing antifreeze out of the overflow line. The truck stopped with the overflow line just above Stinky's navel. Stinky lay there for a moment checking to see if he was hurt, not noticing the green liquid soaking into his coat and two shirts, then it 'reached skin and Stinky began to howl.

"AAAAAAAAAAAAAAAAAAAEEEEEEEEEEEEEEEEEEEEEE."

"That's the noise from the cemetery!" Jonas jumped out of the back of the truck and ran over to the curb, staring wildly about.

"Where's Your Pa Boy?" Dora was looking around for Stinky.

"Oh. Oh. Oh. OOOOOOOOOOOHHHHHHHHHH!" Stinky was using his stocking feet to try and push off the bottom of the bread truck to get himself clear of the scalding stream of antifreeze. He reached a convenient pushing point and unaware it was the crossover for the exhaust pipe on the big V8 engine on the bread truck. The heat melted the nylon in his socks to the bottom of his feet.

"It's the noise from the cemetery Ma." Jonas was backing down the street watching the truck warily and covering his ears each time Stinky let out a wail.

Stinky jerked his feet loose and reached overhead to pull himself with his hands and grabbed the tailpipe on his own truck. He yanked his hands off the pipe then grabbed the cross member on the back of the engine in stead. He pulled himself over toward the left side of the truck and wedged his chest under the transmission, yanked a little harder to pull clear, and he had a tremendous pain in his chest. It was on the left side right where his pocket was. He scooted on out from under the truck and sat up holding his hand up to his chest. He looked down inside his shirts and saw a red half ring of teeth marks oozing blood. He felt his teeth in his pocket, and realized when he had wedged under the transmission he had bitten himself with his false teeth.

He pulled the teeth from his pocket and stuck them back in his mouth, working them around until they sat just right.

Dora was trying to apologize to Lew Maxwell who had decided his truck wasn't hurt and was impatient to get going. Cars were passing around them, drivers gawking at the accident, and Lew was getting later and later on his route. Lew was sure this wreck wouldn't have happened if he hadn't been late getting away from the L&M, all because Enos Mack was late with his morning doughnuts and was slow receiving and signing the ticket for the fresh bread off Lew's truck this morning.

"Sorry Lew. We don't mean to wreck your truck." Stinky walked around to survey the damage, his hand inside his shirt feeling the bite marks.

"It ain't hurt Stinky." Lew was ready to leave. "Your wife pulled out in front o' me Stinky, and my truck ain't hurt. I won't call the cops if you want and we'll just go on."

"OK Lew, if you won't get in no trouble. I don't want no trouble with Junge Bread. They make good bread Lew. I eat lot's o' Bunny Bread don't we Dora." Stinky was ready to go on too, if Lew was willing. Dora didn't have a current driver's license and his truck tag was out of date. Stinky didn't realize that the police in town knew, and chose to look the other way. They didn't want the cost of trash pickup to go up.

"All right Stinky. I'll go on." Stinky leaned over next to the big truck looking where it sat up against his old Dodge, relieved that Lew was so reasonable. Lew climbed in the bread truck, and watching in his big mirrors, he backed up. The truck seemed to back up hard and Lew looked forward and to his surprise Stinky's truck was coming right along with him and Stinky was nowhere to be seen. Lew jerked the truck backwards hoping to shake Stinky's truck loose.

"AAAAAAAAAAAAAAAAAAAEEEEEEEEEEE" Stinky hadn't expected his truck to take off side ways and had hesitated while leaned over to rub the bottom of his foot where it was burnt.

Lew looked out his door with surprise at the sound and saw a furry cap sticking out from under Stinky's truck. "Are you under there again Stinky?" Lew shouted out the door. "Get out o' there Stinky till I shake her loose."

Stinky drug himself out from under his truck and stood, slowly pulling himself up by the mirror bracket and limped over to the curb. Lew jerked the truck back and forth a few times and his bumper disentangled itself from Stinky's truck. Lew waved, drove around Stinky's truck and went south down Garrison.

Stinky climbed back into the truck, where Dora had another cigarette rolled and lit. She had only been mildly annoyed by the jarring and jerking of Lew getting his truck torn loose. She had found a real cigarette paper blowing down the gutter on Garrison and was making quick use of it.

"Get in the truck boy." Stinky shouted out the window of the truck at Jonas who was now standing on the corner watching the lights change.

"Do I got to Pa? It makes awful sounds sometimes Pa." Jonas was looking with some trepidation at the truck.

"Get in the truck boy. OK. Dora let's go." Stinky was watching the traffic.

"Truck won't go Elroy." Dora was stepping on the starter pedal but nothing happened.

Stinky climbed out of the truck and started to get underneath. Then climbed back in the truck, turned off the ignition, took out the key then jammed the gear shift lever into first. "Don't touch the starter pedal Dora till I get back in the truck."

He climbed under the truck wiggled the wires then climbed back up in the cab slamming the now badly deformed door and giving the key back to Dora. She put the key in the truck, turned it on, and stepped on the starter pedal. Much to Stinky's relief the truck started right up.

Dora slipped the truck into low and started around the corner swinging wide left and bouncing off the center median in the center of Chestnut on the east side of Garrison.

When she hit the curb Stinky's door popped open and the centrifugal force of the left turn propelled him out of the truck and into the west bound lane of Chestnut.

"Elroy where you going?" Dora pumped the brakes and lurched to a stop.

113

Stinky picked himself up and climbed in the truck again. "Let's go Dora." Stinky leaned away from the door and the truck rattled north on Garrison.

Dora got the truck in third gear just about sixth street and was going to hit the Oak street light green. Suddenly the view in front of the truck was obscured entirely by the right hood of the truck flopping up and slamming against the windshield. Stinky had the hood on that side open when the truck had started back on Chestnut and Lew's truck had knocked it down but it hadn't been wired down.

At first Dora didn't seem to notice.

"Dora!" Stinky was craning around trying to look out the window without the door coming open. Dora swerved across the left lane and crashed up the curb in front of Winston's Market knocking over an open sign before lurching to a stop just a step short of the wooden front porch. At the abrupt stop, Stinky's door shot open and he hung on tight as it slammed open then bounced back shut against both his shins.

"I can't see Elroy." Dora had dropped her cigarette again and was feeling around for it on the floor of the truck.

Stinky leaned down and rubbed the front of his legs, the pain in his shins completely obliterating the burning on the bottom of his feet in its intensity. He limped around the door, pulled the hood down and made sure it was wired securely.

"Stinky you OK?" Albert Royer came out of the store looking at the truck. "You hit my sign?" Albert walked out to the curb, picked up the sign and looked it over. "It don't look hurt Stinky."

Stinky was back to leaning over inspecting his shins. "Sorry Albert. Hood come open. Couldn't see."

"Lands Stinky, you need to be more careful. I coulda had customers out here." Albert set the sign back over near the corner. "Say Stinky I got somethin' for you to haul off if you'll come back after your route with the truck empty. I'll pay you extree"

"OK Albert. May be a little late." Stinky was craning up to look at the courthouse clock.

"Well be careful getting off the sidewalk." Albert was looking doubtfully at Dora.

Stinky looked up the street and up by the library was a familiar figure.

"You runned off again Pa. I seed you run up the sidewalk Pa. I think I like you runnin' off if yous gonna run up sidewalks." Jonas was shouting and dodging cars on his way up Garrison.

Stinky watched him come "Get in the truck Boy."

"Did it make that noise when it run up the curb Pa? I don't like that noise Pa. It don't sound like no noise a truck oughter make Pa." Jonas really didn't want left behind any more. He couldn't imagine how it kept happening.

"Get in the truck Boy." Stinky rattled the hood one more time, climbed into the passenger seat pulled the door shut and tested his weight against it then thought better of it and just scooted away from the door a ways. "Let's go Dora."

Dora started the truck, looked backwards and let out on the clutch. The truck lurched forward and bounced off the porch of the store before it stopped. Dora hurriedly stuck the truck in reverse, restarted the engine and backed out into a line of traffic. The truck bounced off the curb, slipping in between a southbound Camel freight truck, and mailman Ed Foley in a Jeep. It was a close shave. Dora stopped with the truck heading north in the northbound lane and was very nearly rear ended by Lew Maxwell in the Junge Bread truck.

Lew stomped on the brakes, laid on the horn, and shouted rudely. He had mashed a rack of bread earlier when he hit Stinky's truck he just hadn't noticed till his next stop. Now he heard racks sliding in the back of his truck and he knew it was happening again.

Dora calmly put the truck in low and pulled up to the red light at fourth street. Lew Maxwell followed along behind fuming and cursing. Lew wanted to turn right to go back up to the square, but Dora had the truck straddling the turn lane and the bread truck wouldn't fit in between the truck and the curb. Dora was, as always, fumbling with a cigarette trying to keep it going. The paper or tobacco or something must have been damp. She pulled out when the light turned green nearly sideswiping a car carrier at the Wainford's Ford dealership while smoking and shifting at the same time. Stinky was scooched away from the door to prevent any more unwanted exits and when she crowded the truck at Wainsford's Ford lot, he scooted over closer to Dora.

"What you up to Elroy?" Dora was eying Stinky speculatively

"Watch the light Dora." Stinky was looking at the yellow traffic light soon to be red on Central where she turned east.

"Ask you a question Elroy. What you up to?"

116

When Stinky caught Dora's drift, half a block later, he scooted back closer to the door.

"Turn on Main Dora. I got business with Monty Montgomery." Stinky was thinking about his boots and that anvil.

Dora turned left at Main barely missing a grain truck up from the mill and a car load of women going to the quilting at the Baptist Church. Lucien Wainford was driving one of the brand new Fords from her family dealership and Amanda Adams was in the passenger seat. The preacher's wife from the big Methodist Church was in back with Mrs. Courtney and the word that popped out of the preachers wife's mouth when Dora pulled in front of them was a topic of discussion for months afterward, (whenever she wasn't around anyway).

Two blocks down, and a couple of blocks east, Dora pulled over and parked in front of Monty Montgomery's shop facing the wrong way. Jonas was lying in the back of the truck, on top of the newly collected trash looking at his comic book.

"Jonas! You and your Ma go on out to the dump and empty the truck again." Stinky was peeling off his socks and trying to decide if they were good enough to fix with the big melted holes in the bottom of both feet. A big patch of black sock stayed stuck to both feet when he pulled the socks off. "Come back and get me when you're done unloading."

Monty was pounding steadily on an arm from a three-point hitch from Fred Day's Farmall. Fred had pulled up a rock as big as the tractor with a three point mounted double bottom plow, in, of all places, his mother's garden. It was the same place the garden had been for thirty years and the same tractor and plow they had used for the entire time. The rock was a mystery. Monty heated up the iron arm on the forge then wedged it under a hoop fastened to his bench and pulled on the end with a chain hoist. This secured the arm in place as Monty reshaped the arm in the best way he knew, which was with fire and an eight-pound hammer.

Monty had his back to the door when Stinky stepped in and felt the draft of the forge change so he knew someone was there. "Be right with ya." Monty went on taking to heart the old adage of striking while the iron was hot. He pounded a few more times then dropped the hammer and grabbed the big three point hitch arm and heaved it back onto his forge where he stepped on the handle of the bellows sending up a shower of sparks and heating the big piece of iron to a red glow. He noticed a funny smell, kind of like antifreeze and garbage and without looking knew it had to be Stinky again. He was intent on his work and Stinky stood idly by, waiting. Stinky had been around Monty enough to know there was no point in trying to talk to him while he was working. Stinky kicked around the shop a few minutes poking at things on the floor. He walked over near the forge watching the iron heat up, Monty studying the rosy red color as he scooted the arm in and out of the fire heating a foot long section until it was hot enough to be malleable.

Stinky leaned down and picked up a point from a plow and quickly set it down again. "Hot"

"Yeah" Monty looked at Stinky when he heard the clang of the plow point on the floor. Monty had straightened the plow knife Fred had bent right before he started on the arm.

Stinky watched and became entranced with the process of heating the arm, Monty moving quickly to the anvil pounding some shape into the iron then back to the fire for more heat. The anvil Monty was using really didn't look worn out but Stinky would try to sell him his anvil anyway. Stinky stepped forward just a bit for a better look.

"AAAAAAAAAAAAAAAAAAAEEEEEEEEEEEEEEE" Stinky leapt backward knocking over a row of sickle bars leaning against an iron sawhorse. He was hopping around on one foot fanning the other. The cool bricks of the floor had felt wonderful on his scorched feet and he had forgotten about clinkers always lying about on Monty's floor. Monty raked the impurities out of his coal as he burnt it and scattered them on the floor when he was in a hurry.

Monty nearly lost his hammer and the tractor part when Stinky let out his whoop. "Hot?"

"Hot." Stinky was standing quietly by the door again.

"Where's your shoes?" Monty was studying the spectacle of Stinky, oil, blood, antifreeze, dirt, bare feet and burn marks.

"Left 'em with the anvil." It really didn't occur to Stinky that there was any more explanation needed.

"Well I can take a little break here Stinky. What is it you want? More coffee?" Monty was wiping clinkers and ash out of his cup preparatory to pouring himself a cup. "You already drink all that I gave you?" He was wondering if Stinky had noticed the coffee had chips and dirt in it, but that was almost inconceivable.

"Got me an anvil. I wanna sell it." Stinky never put a price on anything he always waited for an offer. "Gimme anythin' fer it?"

"Well now I gotta see it to know. How big is it? Like mine or bigger?" Monty patted his big anvil sitting on a huge blackened locust stump.

"Maybe bout the same." Stinky held up his hands the perfect picture of the way Jonas had done earlier. "Not quite so big maybe."

"Well is all the corners beat offn it and the top pinged up and the holes for the hardys all fouled and ruint?" Monty didn't really figure Stinky knew.

"Well" Stinky hesitated, "She's heavy."

"Well how do I know if I want it. My Mother in law is heavy and so is my wife but I don't want my Mother-in-law but I'm kinder fond o' my wife." Monty took a drink of his coffee enjoying the body and the strong coffee smell.

"You can see it." Stinky was a little lost.

"Well show it to me then, but I don't want to go too long this here arm ain't done and Fred is a needin it." Monty started toward the door.

"It ain't here." Stinky was thinking hard.

"Well then how can I see it? Can I use binee-ocolars, maybe a teleescope." Monty was baiting Stinky now.

"She's on Chestnut." Stinky was worrying that if he told Monty it was in the trash he wouldn't pay him anything for it.

"Well I cain't see to Chestnut from here." Monty pulled out his big bandana wiped off his face, then cleaned his thick pitted work

120

glasses. He put one glove on his left hand and picked the tractor arm back up.

"That anvil is a sitten at Wolford's house. Out on Chestnut." Stinky was wondering about his boots. "It's out by the curb, with my boots."

"What the heck has your boots got to do with Wolford's anvil that you are a tryin' to sell to me?" Monty had become more and more curious as he studied the way Stinky looked.

"Reckon I left em there." Again this seemed like enough explanation to Stinky.

"Well durned if I unerstan' that, but I'll take a look at yer anvil this afternoon." Monty put the big tractor arm back over the forge and began to step on the bellows handle again.

"You gimme sumpin' fer it?" Stinky was worried now.

"Stinky if I wants it, I'll pay yer somethin' fair fer it!" Monty pulled the arm out of the fire picked up the hammer and began to whang away.

Stinky feeling better about the deal, turned, opened the door and fell over the sill which stood up about six inches above the floor, just like his at home. He picked himself up, nursing a sore toe and started down the street and around the corner to get him some other shoes to wear till Monty moved the anvil. He earnestly hoped Monty took the anvil just so he could get his boots back.

As Stinky rounded the corner he heard the big doors opening on Monty's shop. Funny it still seemed a little cold to open up the doors. Come to think of it he had opened them earlier when he left too.

Stinky rounded the corner to the house, but Dora and Jonas weren't back yet. Stinky went around to the back of the house to wash off his hands in the rain barrel. The sun was up nicely, the sky was blue, the grass had dried out and Stinky was looking up at the sky when he stepped in a rather large gift left by the hound. He jumped when he felt it squish up between his toes and landed on a toy truck Jonas had brought home from the dump for his nephews and nieces to play with. Stinky's foot just fit in the metal bed of the toy truck mashing his toes thoroughly in the process. He stood on one foot and dislodged the toy from his other then went on to the rain barrel not looking anywhere but where he was stepping. Stinky pulled up an old metal kitchen chair that had the back missing and climbed up on it so he could dip his foot in the barrel to clean it off. Stinky got his right foot in the barrel and his left foot went through the seat of the chair dropping him astraddle the side of the barrel with his toes just inches above the ground and the bottom of the barrel. He reached out with his right hand to grab the edge of the barrel and missed, his hand sliding down the inside of the big wooden barrel and his neck landing on the far edge. Stinky rolled to his right and fell off the top of the barrel leaving his leg inside to hang him upside down when his foot wedged under the other edge of the barrel hoop where a lid was once attached. David Jr. came out the back door to see what the noise was and saw a fearful sight of a monster crawling out of the rain barrel and ran into the house.

"AAAAAAAAAAAAAAEEEEEEEEEEEEE" David sounded just like Stinky.

Dora and Jonas had just pulled up in front of the house and Jonas heard the sound. "There it is Ma! There is that sound Ma. I don't like that sound Ma. You hear it Ma?" Jonas was glad the sound had quit coming from the truck but what if it kept up coming from the house, maybe even at night. Jonas shuddered.

Stinky got his foot untangled and fell to the ground next to the rain-barrel. His foot was cleaner anyway. He went inside the house and rummaged around in the corner of the kitchen where he thought he had seen a sock but all he found was one of those socks a baseball player wears over regular socks, with just a stirrup under your foot.

Dora came in and began rummaging around in the kitchen cabinets looking for another Prince Albert can. She had found the trash sacks from the VFW out at the dump, and needed more storage for the cigarette butts.

"Dora you seen any socks?" Stinky didn't really expect Dora to know. Marcia washed clothes sometimes. Maybe she would know. But the house was empty except for the hound, which had crept down off Stinky's and Dora's bed when he heard someone coming and was now lounging back on Grandma's pallet in the corner.

"Pa did you hear that sound? It was like the Cemetery Pa. I hearded it up at the corner where Lew hit our truck too. It's a arful sound ain't it Pa?" Jonas was rummaging around in some bread sacks and eating the heals out of the bottom.

"I need socks." Stinky gave up asking Dora.

"You need socks Pa? I got socks. I'm wearin' socks Pa. I got lots of socks Pa. Snakes don't wear socks Pa. Maybe a snake ud wear jus one sock?" Jonas fell into deep thought and was just about to drown.

"Well where are they?" Stinky's feet were hurting and were cold. No-one had ever built a fire in the stove.

"In the dry sink. I stores 'em there so's I don't loose em. I got lots of socks. Lots." Jonas went over and was rummaging around in dirty dishes and the dish pans and pulling out socks of all colors.

"They look a mite small for me don't they Boy?" Stinky was eying the socks Jonas was pulling out.

"These here is David's socks. I share my place with David. They used ter be Raymond's socks and some of them used to be my socks and some was Michaels. They was little then, so wuz I. Little when I wored em. They is gettin' kinder wore lookin ain't they? I couldn't wear them no more." Jonas was studying the socks

"You got socks to fit me?" Stinky was contemplating those little worn out socks, and the feet that used to fit in them.

"Sure I got socks. I got lots of socks" Finally Jonas pulled out one blue sock with a hole in the heel that looked like it might be big enough for Stinky. Then he pulled out a green plaid sock that had a lump in the toe that wiggled. Jonas dropped it quick and the frighted mouse charged out of his disturbed nest and ran under some rags in the corner of the kitchen.

The hound who was now drowsing under the kitchen table saw the mouse and charged after it. The dog knocked the board holding up one corner of the table and it turned over spilling it's contents across the floor, including the pot of beans from the day before. The pot edge landed on Stinky's left foot causing him to hop in circles holding on to his toes. This distracted the hound and he turned his attention to lapping up the beans. Stinky shooed him away and pushed part of the spilled beans back into the big pot and set it back upright.

"Found you another sock Pa. It ain't just the same Pa. It has some holes in it too." Jonas was studying a red sock somewhat doubtfully.

"Gimme them socks boy." Stinky wasn't paying attention and the hound had come back and was wolfing down beans out of the big pot. "Get out o' there you dog." Stinky propped the table back up on it's board and put the pot of beans back up on the table.

Stinky pulled on the socks putting the hole in the heel around on top on the blue one and arranging the red sock so none of his toes stuck through. It had lots of little moth holes in it. Then Stinky remembered that sock. Back about last new year, Stinky had figured that the truck battery might stay charged up all night if he kept it inside, where it was warmer. He had set it by the stove, and then stoked up the fire crawled in bed with Ma, and went to sleep. Michael, his number four son, had woken up, and the battery had been hissing and puffing, and Michael, fearing an imminent explosion, carried it over and threw it out the front door. When Stinky got up in the morning and went to stand by the stove, the acid that had spewed out of the battery and onto the floor, ate holes through his sock. He had thrown the worst one out. Or maybe this was the bad one, and he had lost the other one.

Stinky went into the front room and rummaged around looking for another pair of shoes that would fit him. There was a wingtip shoe in the corner but there didn't seem to be any match to it.

Stinky thought about it for a bit, and went out to the outhouse. Up high in the peak of the roof was a boot, hanging from a nail. Stinky climbed up on the edge of the seat and reached up and pulled the boot down. It was a pull on boot. There was a starling's nest in the boot, unoccupied at this time of the year. Stinky climbed down carefully sat down and pulled the boot on his right foot. He went to the crawl space hole under his house and pulled a lace-up boot out from under the foundation, banged it against the wall of the house to shake the occupants out and pulled it on. It fit a little strangely. Looked funny too. Well it was better than socks only.

"Let's go Dora." Stinky headed around the house, his gait rather stilted by the odd boot combination.

"I'm eatin'." Dora was shoveling beans into her mouth from the pot on the table. Ashes from her cigarette falling into the beans with each trip of the spoon, from pot to mouth.

Stinky went around to the truck, climbed in the passenger side, and relaxed in the warm sun. His wet clothes steamed and fumed in the warm cab. He leaned his head back and rested against the back window. Jonas was lying in the papers left in the back of the truck watching clouds way up high, drifting prettily along. He never imagined them to be anything like animals or people or anything of that sort. They were just clouds to Jonas. It was warm and nice in the sun in the back of the truck.

When Dora came out of the house wiping beans from around her mouth with the front of her shirt, the truck was rolling quietly down the hill toward the corner. Stinky must have decided to go on without her. She turned and walked back in the front door to eat more beans. "The beans were about all gone anyway, so she might as well finish them off."

Stinky woke up just in time to see the truck mow down the stop sign at the corner. Jonas woke up at the crash, thinking they were heading back out on the route and not noticing they were up on the sidewalk and about a foot from the wall of the Lawson Grocery Warehouse again. Jonas pulled out his comic book and opened it up as the truck careened across the street.

Fred Day, on his way to the blacksmith shop, just missed Stinky's truck by yanking the wheel on the big grain truck to the side and nearly turning it over in the middle of the street. Monty heard the honking and the tires squealing, and walked out to the sidewalk to see what the racket was about. (His big doors were still open.) Fred nearly ran Monty down looking in his big side mirror and cursing at Stinky.

Stinky's truck missed the curb by a whisker on the east side of the street and started down the next block before he could get scooted across the seat and his foot planted on the brake. He steered the truck toward the center of the street and pumped frantically at the brake pedal. Nothing happened. The truck continued to pick up speed. He tried hard to jam the truck into gear to slow it down but there was no provision for such a maneuver in the old Dodge. Synchronizers were unheard of when it was built.

He yanked on the parking brake, knowing it hadn't worked in years. It was a big hand lever and Stinky grabbed it with both hands and heaved. It pulled further than he thought it was supposed to go and the right rear tire locked up, lurching the truck around sideways and throwing Stinky against the left door, which promptly came open and spat him out upon the ground. He landed on all fours on the asphalt road. Jonas had slid around in the back of the truck and half the load of paper had slid over the top of him burying him in trash. (He and Dora had done a poor job of unloading.) Stinky picked himself up and crawled back into the cab and then remembered the brakes and got back out. He unwired the left side hood and pushed it open. He reached in under the hood and pulled the little wire bail that held the master cylinder for the brakes closed. He pulled off the lid and then pulled the rubber gasket loose. It looked dry in there.

"Did the hood come up again Pa? Didja bout crash the truck Pa? Is the truck broke now Pa?" Jonas was standing in the bed peering over the cab of the truck.

"Out of brake oil." Stinky went back to the cab and begun rummaging around under the seat. Used motor oil didn't work good in the brakes. He had found that out from fat Leopold when Leopold put it in his Hudson Hornet. It had worked until Leopold had got the car out of town and out on the highway headed toward the Golden Door. Stinky and Jonas had picked parts of that car up for a hundred yards after he missed the corner where the road went from four lanes to two lanes. Leopold had run that Hornet through the go-cart track and under the railroad overpass before stopping on the tracks.

"Brake Oil? Ain't oil slick? I stepped in oil oncet and fell down. Course it was cooking oil. It'd run out of the garbage at the L&M. It smelled like french fries. Oil 'ud make the brakes slippy wouldn't it Pa? I wouldn't like slippy brakes. You want the brakes should smell like french fries? We might go in front of Lew's bread truck again and he would pop us one. I don't want no slippy brakes if Lew is gonna bang into us again." Jonas was thinking out loud.

Stinky gave up on the truck and began walking west back up the hill. "Stay with the truck boy." Monty would have brake oil.

Jonas threw himself back down in the trash and stretched out on his back in the sun to read his comic.

Stinky walked back up the hill and saw that there was a truck in front of Monty's. Looked kind of familiar. He crossed the street and entered Monty's shop. Monty was back at his desk writing up a bill for Fred Day. Fred had his back to Stinky but turned around as soon as the air wafted his direction.

"Need some brake erl." Stinky was looking past Fred at Monty.

"Hold on Stinky I gotta take care o' business here first" Monty noticed Fred's discomfiture. "Wait over by the door."

Fred signed the bill at the bottom and picked up the plow knife. Monty put on his gloves, hefted the three-point hitch arm and headed for the truck. Stinky was standing facing out of the big doors and Monty crowded him with the big piece of hot iron and dragged it across Stinky's backside. You could smell the cloth singe.

Stinky jumped and scooted out the door and across the sidewalk. "Hot"

"Yeah. Hot." Monty grunted as he heaved the arm into Fred's truck.

"See Ya Sunday Monty." This indicated either, fishing, hunting (quail, dove, deer) trot line, football (watching) baseball (watching)

129

or church (sleeping). Fred climbed in his truck and roared off, trailing blue smoke.

"What you doin' here again Stinky?" Monty headed for a cup of coffee and the remains of a sandwich he hadn't finished.

"Need some brake erl." Stinky was eying Monty's sandwich.

"You mean hydraulic brake fluid?" Monty was ignoring Stinky's hungry look.

"Yeah. Brake erl" Stinky was surreptitiously slavering.

"How much you need?" Monty finished off his sandwich.

"'Nough to fill up my truck." Stinky was crestfallen as the last of the sandwich disappeared.

"You mean the master cylinder is empty?" Monty pulled out a couple of Hostess Snowballs and unwrapped them, careful to hold them by the wrapper to keep them clean.

"Brakes ain't workin'." Stinky rubbed his hand across the back of his mouth to prevent obvious drooling.

"I got some over there by the side door in a pint can. Up on the shelf." Monty had polished off the first snowball in one big bite.

Stinky went over to the side door and pulled down a can. "Much 'bliged"

"Mmmmhumm" Monty was busy finishing off his second snowball, trying to keep the marshmallow off his face.

Stinky headed back down to his truck as Monty went out back to wash off at the pump.

Stinky carefully poured the fluid into the brake reservoir and put the cap back on. He climbed into the truck and pumped the brake a couple of times.

After a few seconds of pumping the pedal firmed up and felt like the truck had brakes again. He started up the truck and started to take off, but the truck just moaned and died when he let out the clutch. That was when he noticed the hand brake lever was still pulled out. He grabbed the lever and pushed but nothing happened. He then latched onto the lever with both hands and heaved it back into it's place. He started up the truck and tried again but the truck still wouldn't move. He climbed out of the truck and looked underneath. The hand brake cable was hanging down almost to the ground. Stinky crawled under the truck and began yanking on the cable. After a tug or two He thought better of it and climbed back out.

"Hey boy get out o' the truck and come round here."

"I'm readin' a comic Pa. You wanna read it Pa? Snakeses cain't read can they Pa?" Jonas was looking through the slats of the truck.

"Come out here boy and hold your foot on the brake." Stinky figured it was safer to have Jonas hold the brake than trust the engine compression to hold the truck still when he got the hand brake cable released.

"Am I gonna drive Pa? I don't think I oughter drive Pa. I ain't got no register to drive Pa. I learned in school; You gotter have a register to drive." Jonas was reticent about getting in the truck.

"You ain't gonna drive. Just hold your foot on the brake." Stinky was crawling back under the truck. "Get in the truck boy."

"I don't want no Police to grab me fer drivin' Pa. I ain't got a register." Jonas hung off the tailgate head down peering under at Stinky.

"You ain't gonna drive. You don't need no register." Stinky was studying the cable to see what was hung up.

"If I don't need no register why does you and Ma have to haff a register." Jonas knew when he was right.

"We ain't got no register. We got a license." Stinky thought he had found the problem.

"I ain't got a license Pa." Jonas was beginning to sulk "I ain't got no register neither."

"Get in the truck boy. You ain't gonna drive." Stinky found the problem for sure "Hold your foot on the brake."

"Will you come see me if the police get me and put me in the hoosegow?" Jonas climbed out of the truck and was shouting down at Stinky.

"Get in the truck boy." Stinky was ready to release the cable.

"I pushed the pedal down hard Pa." Jonas was making engine sounds and twisting the steering wheel back and forth. "MMMMMMMMMMMMMMM Mbrrrrrrrrbrrrrr" It was safe enough to do that, he could turn the steering wheel half a turn and it had no effect on the front wheels.

"Hold the pedal down good boy." Stinky yanked the cable down and it snapped back up tight releasing the brake and the truck began to roll down the hill. Stinky yanked his feet in under the truck to keep the tires from hitting him. "Push on the brake boy!"

"The truck is movin' Pa! I's gonna get throwed in the hoosegow! I ain't got no register." Jonas was almost ready to cry.

"Push on the brake boy!" The truck had almost cleared Stinky when the hole in the shin of his pants caught on the iron channel that was the rear bumper.

"AAAAAAAAAAAAAAArrrrggg Push on the brake Boy!"

"There's that sound Pa! Help Pa." The truck was picking up speed and Jonas was thinking about bailing out.

"Pump ughh the urf pedal oh!" Stinky was bouncing down the road. Even though not moving very fast it was hard to keep your head from bouncing on the street.

"Help Pa she won't stop." Jonas was pushing on the pedal till his face was turning red.

"Pump. Pump!" The truck was still rolling slowly but the hill was getting steeper.

"I ain't got no pump Pa!" Jonas was looking about wildly.

"Let off the pedal oooff" Stinky was going to continue "And push it down again." But, his voice was drowned out by the truck engine starting.

"What are you doing boy!" Then it dawned on Stinky "Push on both pedals boy! Both pedals!"

"Help Pa." Jonas was pumping the pedal, the clutch pedal, and the truck was lurching violently. "I'm pushing Pa. I don't wanna be throwed in the hoosegow."

"Push both pedals boy." Stinky was being bounced with every push of the clutch.

Jonas pushed on the gas pedal and the clutch pedal together and the truck roared horribly scaring him even more by backfiring when he let off the gas. Flames shot out of the exhaust scaring Stinky as well. Next Jonas pushed on the gas and the brake together which made the truck speed up, the engine being stronger than the brakes. Then he stomped on the starter pedal and the gas together which made the truck speed up and a terrible screeching sound. "It's a siren Pa. They gonna get me!"

Stinky opened his eyes after the blast of the backfire and saw that they were about to plow the curb on the left side of the road where a big brick building that used to house a carriage works stood. "Turn boy! Look out! Turn!"

Jonas looked up from his wild stomping on the pedals to see the building bearing down on him. He wrenched the wheel to the right and nothing happened then to the left and the truck bounced up the curb just missing the corner of the building and taking down the stop sign. Stinky swung a little to the right with centrifugal force and just grazed the corner of the curb catching his sweater he was wearing under his coat by the waist on the bent over stub of the stop sign. After a short tug of war, much to his dismay, his pants won the battle and his sweater began ripping off from under his coat, leaving his sleeves in tact and his pant leg still hooked to the truck. Jonas steered further right and the truck was off, heading north, down toward the mill.

"AAAAAAAAAAAArgggggghhhh", Stinky was being squeezed by the sweater being ripped from under his coat. "Push on the brake boy!"

Jonas couldn't hear Stinky at all now, but he had learned by repeated tries which combinations of pedals made terrible sounds. "Help Pa!"

Jonas pulled his feet up into the seat afraid to push on any more pedals since everything had been wrong so far. In pulling up his legs he knocked the truck out of gear, which caused the truck to go faster in a free roll than it had been when idling in first gear. Jonas saw the raised sidewalk looming up in front of him and the wall that supported it getting too close on the left. He jerked the wheel to the right swinging Stinky around to where he could nearly reach the bolt where his pants were hooked. Then the big stone railroad bridge abutment on the right started flying toward Jonas and he jerked the wheel back to the left moving Stinky back out of reach of the offending bolt. Stinky's outer pair of pants were beginning to work down, but he didn't want to be drug on down the street on just his inside pair of pants so he grabbed onto the waist of his pants and hung on. Jonas decided on one more chance and grabbed the hand brake and heaved. The lever came back, the truck skidded right with the right rear tire locked up then the lever came off in Jonas's hand causing the truck to coast slowly down to the bottom of the hill and bump gently into the raised sidewalk on the west side of the road directly below the railroad overpass. Stinky was relieved the truck had stopped and was untangling his pant leg. Jonas didn't know where his Pa was, but he was getting away from the truck, which was still idling.

The driver's side door had been slammed shut when they had bounced over the curb and now it wouldn't come open. The passenger door had been bouncing open and shut as they wandered down the road and was standing open. Just as Jonas climbed out of the truck, the one o'clock west bound freight blew its air horn and roared overhead. Jonas threw himself on the ground in fear, holding his hands over his ears till the train passed.

"Pa where did you go?" Jonas was looking accusingly at Stinky sitting behind the truck. "You gonna get me thrown in the hoosegow Pa. You think I'm the snake Pa? You think snakes ought ta be in the hoosegow Pa? Where is your boot Pa? You gonna leave all your boots like the ones with the iron thing?

Stinky unwound his pant leg then stood up and tugged his pants back into position. He looked back up the street and saw a sock and further up near the corner lay his boot. "Get my boot for me boy, and my sock"

Jonas trotted back up the street while Stinky took off his coat and pulled the sleeves and the collar of his sweater off.

"You want the string Pa?" Jonas was studying a wadded tangle of yarn strung out between the signpost and Stinky's truck. "You know how to knit Pa? Think Gramma would knit sumpin' If'n I saved it? It's mighty tangley ain't it. Kinder like a cat furball only not so tight. It kinder looks like your sweater Pa."

"Bring me my boot boy." Stinky's foot was getting cold, "And my sock."

"We could make you a sock outen this here string Pa ifn I had knittin' needles." Jonas was still studying the wad of string. "It'ld take me a bit though. Knots is a problem in knittin'. I mean making knots is a problem. I mean not tyin' knots but having knots just sorta get in the string. That real fuzzy string is the worst."

"Bring my boot, boy, and my sock." Stinky was standing on one foot and studying the worn through elbows of his coat.

"Want the String Pa? I brung the string." Jonas finally delivered the boot and the sock.

Jonas handed Stinky the boot first which he started to put on then stopped and grabbed the sock away from Jonas and pulled it on first only to discover that it was now a tube, not a sock. Stinky folded the open end under his toes and pulled on his boot. The boots still didn't look right. It wasn't just that one was a lace up and one was a pull on. They just didn't look right to Stinky.

"Do my boots look funny boy?" Stinky stood staring down at his feet.

"Sure Pa. One boot don't look like the other one does." Jonas Studied on it for a piece before he decided that was it. "Yup. One's got strings."

"Hum. That ain't it." Stinky started to get in the driver side and found the door blocked shut by the retaining wall below the trestle.

"This your sweater in the back Pa? Looks like you oughter keep that string and make you a new un." Jonas held up the remains of Stinky's sweater, which Stinky had thrown in the back of the truck. There were the sleeves and collar attached to each other at the shoulder but no torso.

"Get in the truck boy." Stinky walked around behind the truck and climbed in the passenger side. He slammed the door and it promptly bounced back open. Stinky pulled the door to and found it wouldn't come shut. He studied the latch a bit, got his jug of oil out from behind the truck seat and poured some into the mechanism. He didn't notice the oil running out of the door bottom and into his lace up boot. Stinky put the jug away stuffing the rag back in the top, the same one he strained the oil with before putting it in the truck, and climbed in again. He pulled the door to and it latched.

"Are we goin' without Ma?" Jonas was standing in the bed of the truck leaning around and down toward Stinky's window. "I cain't drive no more till I get a register. Can I get a register Pa? Leopold says he learned to drive when he was twelve and I's older than twelve. I'm near seventeen. Am I old enough to get a register Pa?"

"You don't need no register. You gotta take a test and get a driver's license." Stinky put the truck in reverse and backed away from the wall.

"A test? I ain't good at tests. That's why I ain't in school no more cause I done poorly at tests. Tests is mean hard uncomfortable." Jonas was very disappointed. "I guess I don't need no register."

Stinky turned around in the bedspring factory driveway and went back up the hill toward his house, testing the brakes to make sure they worked. They felt kind of mushy but not too bad. He pulled the truck up in front of his house and Jonas jumped out and deftly slipped the board under the wheel on the downhill side and Stinky shut off the truck.

"Go find your Ma." Stinky was going to relax in the cab for a bit and take stock of his sore spots.

Jonas went in the front door looking around for his Ma. Marcia and the baby were listening to the radio and were sitting right up in front of it. The lantern battery they ran it from was about dead. Even old lantern batteries had enough juice to run the radio for a while. They would have to look for more old batteries in the dump. Fat Leopold always stuck his wallet chain across the battery posts to see if it would spark. If it would spark it was good enough to run the radio a while. Stinky had one blow up like that once, so he just took them home and tried them out.

Jonas went out to the kitchen and found his Ma leaning back against the counter in a three legged chair, finishing off the beans. "Pa says we gonna finish the route now, and since I ain't got no register I don't get to drive no more."

"I gotta get me a drink first" Ma was looking at the water bucket, which was sitting by the drysink. There was no dipper and the bucket had leaked down to a puddle in the bottom. Dora picked up the bucket and drank what was left out of the bottom. "Lemme get my cigarette makins"

" Pa says ifn I wants a register I gotta take a test. I don' want no tests. That's why I don't go ta school any more. I done poorly on a test. Maybe I wont do poorly on a test fer a register. Then I could drive Pa round the route and he could ride in the back or in the truck with me." Jonas picked up Ma's freshly cut cigarette papers and her can and he and Dora headed out for the truck.

Stinky had pulled out his peanuts and was munching contentedly. He gave Jonas a handful of peanuts and then a shake of Crackerjacks and they were ready to go. "Get in the truck boy."

Jonas climbed in the truck bed, Dora got in the passenger side. Stinky started the truck then waited. "Pull out the board boy." He shouted out the window.

"I'm in the truck Pa." Jonas looked over the slats in Stinky's window.

"Well pull out the board, then get in the truck." Stinky was becoming worried about ever finishing their route.

Jonas pulled the board out from under the wheel and Stinky waited till he had climbed in the back of the truck and started off again. Dora had a full stomach and plenty of "makins" so she was happy. Jonas had eaten a few of the peanuts and Crackerjacks and had gotten the last swallow of Stinky's Grapette and had his comic. They drove back down to Chestnut and started west back to the route. Stinky turned around at the store and aimed the truck back east. He stopped next door to Wolfords' where the anvil and his boots were still sitting.

"Scoot over here and drive Dora." Stinky was climbing out of the driver side door which protested with loud screeches and groans. "We gotta get a move on, We's late."

"You want I should drive Pa? I can drive even though I ain't gotta register if you says I can. Marcia says you taught Leopold ta drive. Snakeses cain't drive."

"Just pick up the trash boy." Stinky picked up a can and got started.

They worked along steady, not spending the time they normally would scrutinizing the trash. "What if we miss sumpin" good Pa? 'Member that dollar Leopold found oncet? He boughted us icecream. What if we miss a dollar Pa? What if we miss two dollars?"

"Just keep on workin' boy. We gotta hustle if we want Marvin ta pay us today." Stinky was hoping Marvin hadn't been down Chestnut and seen how late they were or worse yet, he hoped no one had called to complain. Marvin might dock their pay, or take their anvil or something.

The day had been warming up nicely till nearly three thirty when clouds began to roll in. A big black line that stretched from the north-east to the south west began to creep into view. The sun shot it's rays over the tops of the clouds and made the edges bright silver. Stinky was enjoying the view without deducing what those black clouds portended.

"Pa. Look the silver linin's is a leakin' out o' them clouds. Ain't that sumpin' Pa?" Jonas was staring at the clouds in fascination.

"Ya boy, it's sumpin'" Stinky was still impatient to keep moving, but he spent another moment looking at the sky. "We better hurry."

"OK Pa. Them clouds is comin' fast ain't they Pa." Jonas still stared in fascination.

"We better hurry boy." Stinky had finally made the connection between the clouds and what the weather might do and was thinking more than ever that they better hurry.

The work was going smoothly as they moved up Chestnut almost to Sophia where Stinky felt the first big gust of wind as the cold front moved across. It was a powerful blast, which nearly took the trashcan out of his hands. Paper swirled up from the back of the truck.

"Jonas get up in the truck and stomp it down a bit." Stinky was running across the street. "Jonas get up in the truck and stomp it down!"

"What?" Jonas was cupping his hand around his ear like his Grandpa used to do. "What?" The wind whipped the sound away immediately. "The trash is blowin' away Pa. Want I should hold it down?"

Stinky was pursuing a wildly rolling trashcan down to Sophia. "Dora come on up here." He shouted, but the wind prevented her from hearing so he began to wave frantically to Dora.

Dora saw him motioning and drove east following Stinky. Stinky captured the can and turned around to take it back to it's owner's home when he saw half a dozen more empty trash cans go crashing out into the street. He whirled around just in time to get caught in the back of the knees by a nearly full trashcan from the south side of the street. It bowled him over and bulldozed up his back bouncing up into the air when it hit his head and spilling the remains of it's contents on the ground then flying down into the big drainage ditch they were parked next to. The trees were thrashing wildly and any leaves left from summer were torn away. The new asphalt shingles on the front of Mrs Breackman's house were standing in ranks. Small limbs were beginning to snap off and Stinky figured that bigger ones would start soon. He gave up on corralling the rolling trashcans and ran to the truck. Jonas was spread eagle on the pile of trash in the back o the truck trying to prevent it from sailing out.

"Get in the truck boy." Stinky felt the first big drops as he was attempting to wrench open the driver's door.

"I'm in the truck Pa." Jonas was being pelted by the trash swirling around in the truck bed "I cain't hold 'e r Pa. She's gonna blow about some."

"Get in the cab o' the truck boy it's a gonna rain hard. Maybe hail!" Stinky got the door open and was trying to find the handle to the window, which was normally laying on the dash. He finally found it under the seat. "Not in this side, on the other side." Jonas was waiting to get in the driver's side.

Stinky went on trying to close the window by pulling on the glass and cranking at the same time. The handle kept coming off and he barked his knuckles on the shaft sticking out of the door twice. "Dora give me a hand here."

"I cain't get the door open." Jonas was heaving on the right hand door. "She's stuck Pa." Jonas pulled on the truck so hard it was rocking. The wind was shrieking around them as finally Stinky and Dora got the window rolled up. Stinky crawled in and puled the door partway shut just as Jonas appeared outside his door.

"Lemme in Pa. She's gonna rain cats an' hogs." The big drops were coming down closer together and Jonas was getting wet.

"Get in the truck boy." Stinky climbed out and Jonas climbed in and just sat there. "Scoot over Boy" Stinky was getting wetter than he had been in months. "Let me in."

Dora just sat where she was in the middle so Jonas began to crawl over the top of her. He had nearly made it over when Stinky climbed in and Jonas gave a lunge to get over his mother and kicked Stinky in the face knocking him on his back on the ground.

"You loose sumpin" on the ground Pa? You find money on the ground Pa?" Jonas leaned back over his mother looking at Stinky who was on his hands and knees watching the blood from his nose join the water rushing down the gutter run away in little pink streams. Stinky groggily got up, pulled out his rag, slapped it over his nose and climbed in the truck.

"Didja fall on yer nose again Pa?" Jonas studied Stinky intently. "Don't it hurt Pa?"

"You're a gettin" me wet Elroy. You're drippy." Dora was scooting away from Stinky to avoid the little rivulets flowing off him. "You shouldn't oughter o' got on the ground Elroy. It was wet."

Stinky put the truck in gear and started to drive off, then thought better of it and stopped again. He twisted the knob on the top of the dash that ran the windshield wipers, the engine began to run badly and there was a hissing noise from under the dash. The vacuum line was off the wipers. The rain was coming down in sheets now and the cracked linoleum on the roof of the truck was leaking down Stinky's neck. His nosebleed had, thankfully, slowed to a drip.

"I gotter reach under the dash so scootch over a bit Dora." Dora snuggled over against Stinky. "The other way."

When she had moved away, Stinky leaned over and stuck a hand up under the dash feeling for the bottom of the little valve that

144

ran the wipers. He couldn't reach up high enough so he pulled his feet up onto the seat on the door side and pulled around so he rested his shoulders on the floor of the truck with his feet sticking up. There was rain running in around the windshield and dripping down the dash into his face so he couldn't see, but he thought he could feel the little hose that ran the wipers.

"Watch out Elroy you 'bout kicked my cigarette outen my mouth." Dora was indignant at her cigarette being endangered.

He thrashed around trying to get a better reach without kicking Dora and bumped the window handle, which caused the window to fall down into the door. A river of water began to run off the roof of the truck in the window and down Stinky's pant leg. "Close the winder"

"Why'd you open the winder Elroy?"Dora was scooting Jonas up against the other door trying to avoid the deluge. "You knowed it was a rainin'."

Stinky found the end of the vacuum line and pushed it onto the little wiper valve and was rewarded with the sound of the wiper thumping back and forth overhead. He squirmed around on the floor till he could scramble back up into the seat by climbing all over Dora.

"Elroy you's gettin" me wet." Dora had given up on her cigarette and was clutching her tobacco tins to herself trying to keep them dry.

"Help me get the winder closed again." Stinky had the window handle and was trying to roll the window back up. He got a hold on the top of the glass and on the third try succeeded in pulling it up while Dora cranked till only about a two-inch crack remained at the top. When he tried to pull it up further Dora cranked hard and mashed his fingers, then, the window fell back down leaving a two-inch gap. Stinky pulled a burlap sack used for picking walnuts from under the seat and stuffed it into the crack above the glass. Black stain, the residue of walnut hulls, coursed down the door and ran down Stinky's side and arm. The driver's side windshield wiper was not moving. The passenger side was merrily swinging back and forth with no wiper blade on it. Stinky had hooked the wrong hose to the vacuum valve.

"I still cain't see Pa. and the water's a runnin down my leg. Can we go home Pa?" Jonas hated the cold wet filling his boots. "The trash is all blowed everywhere so's we cain't get it nohow.

Stinky twisted back around and onto the floor of the truck and felt around for the vacuum line he had just connected and yanked it off. He pawed around and found the other hose and stuck it on and heard the wiper begin scraping and scratching back and forth across the glass. He squirmed his way back around without kicking anyone more than twice and looked out through the windshield. Big streaks traveled across the window with each swipe of the wiper and were filled almost as soon as the wiper went by. A tremendous flash and a clap of thunder nearby caused all three of them to jump like they were shot. Then came another flash and crash, and another.

"We better go Elroy. They's gettin' closer to the mark every bang." Dora was getting nervous that the lightning's aim might improve.

" I seed it Pa. It hit ol' Mr Breackman's house. The house glowed Pa. It shone up like fireworks. I seeded it." Jonas was bouncing up and down and shouting excitedly. "It's loud ain't it? Louder than the Fourth o' July."

Stinky put the truck in gear and started to take off, and the windshield wiper stopped moving. He pushed the clutch back in and the wiper scraped away again. He pushed on the gas let out the clutch a bit and the wiper stopped again so he pushed in the clutch again. The wiper took off and worked along steady. This time he killed the engine. Hail was starting to pound on the roof of the truck. At first it was pea size bouncing and rolling, turning the yards white, then larger, acorn size then almost to the size of large grapes.

"It's gonna bust her sure Pa." Jonas was studying the big white projectiles bouncing off the windshield. Lightening struck the power pole just east of where the truck was and balls of fire jumped from the lines and the poles to the nearby trees. "Yoooww eeee! Pow! Did'ja see it. Wow! It was balls o' lightnin'. Wow. Wow. Gee."

Stinky just stared in amazement at the pyrotechnics going on around them. Dora hugged her cigarette tins to herself and squeezed her eyes shut.

"Oh. Oh. Oh. Oh. My."

"It nearly gotted us didn't it Pa. It was a firin' fer us an' missed by a bit. Woweee. Zap! If it ud a got us Pa we'd a looked like that bird got in the transformer on the L&M's neon lights wouldn't we Pa. Wow." Jonas was in awe of the spectacle.

The hail had faded to a spattering of pea size chunks mixed in with a steady downpour of rain.

"Reckon the Raidens are home?" Stinky was looking at the house where they were stopped. "Reckon I better go borry their phone and call somebody that Brinkman's house got struck by lightning."

"They gots a car in the garage Pa." Jonas was looking down the driveway to the single car garage in back. "Reckon Mrs. Breakman is home?"

"I don't know boy. I wouldn't wanna be home for no lightning strike." Stinky, realizing there was nothing for it, jumped out of the truck and ran to the porch of the Raiden house. Just as he reached the porch, another flash of lightning lit the sky, and Stinky bounded to the top of the stairs and slid across the wet limestone porch to crash into the screen door with a bang that even Dora noticed.

Just as Stinky managed to get himself back to his feet, the front door flew open and Fred Raiden stood there glaring out of the screen door. Stinky was inclined to laugh since Fred was in his underwear and a pair of lace up boots, and that was all, but his double barrel twelve gauge looked ready for action. "What the heck Stinky?"

Stinky fought off the urge to run and choked out, "Lightning."

"Lord yes, it's lightning. Why are you up here banging on my house." Fred was looking less likely to shoot him by now, so Stinky finally blurted out.

"Lightning struckeded the Breakman's, I mean Brinkman's."

At that news, Fred stepped behind the door and leaned up the shotgun and came out on the porch for a look. "You sure Stinky?"

At that point, the big fire siren uptown began to wail. "Supose that is for here?" Stinky asked.

"Don't know. I better call and make sure." Fred went back in the house without inviting Stinky in. Just then, the Fire Chief's '55 Pontiac station wagon appeared on Chestnut, coming from the East. His lights were flashing and he was spraying rooster tails out behind the wheels with his speed. Not far behind him was the Ambulance that had just left the Funeral Home up the street and before they arrived, Stinky could hear the unmuffled roar of the fire truck leaving the station up north of the square.

Fred had returned to the door, and said, "Operator said old man Brinkman himself called, and was a mite excited. Guess you ain't going to be the hero today Stinky."

The fire chief and one of his firefighters had leapt out of the car and were circling the house looking for signs of fire. Soon the big red fire truck arrived and the rest of the six man crew swarmed out of the truck, some going inside, some roaming around outside.

All this time, Fred Raiden had been peeking out of the door watching the action, still just wearing his skivvys and his boots. "Reckon I best get back in Stinky. It was good of you to come and tell me to call. You know, gettin' out of your truck and gettin' all wet and all."

Stinky realized the futility of explaining to Fred, and just said, "Sorry 'bout the trash not gettin' picked today." With that, he carefully made his way down the wet slippery steps and back to the truck.

"Didja see it Pa?" Jonas was so excited he could barely contain himself. "Fire trucks!!"

"I saw boy." Stinky allowed himself a grin, "Pretty exciting huh?"

"Yeah Pa! Pretty excitin'." Jonas was squinting through the windshield soaking in every detail. "This is the best day ever!"

Stinky thought that over a minute and let it go. "Guess we better see if they's any cans with garbage that ain't blowed away."

Stinky tried starting the truck and nothing happened.

"The wires is loose again. Reckon we will wait fer the rain to slow down." Stinky had figured on finishing up and going in to Marvin's office but there was no hurry now. "We cain't pick up much more trash today." The truck was in fact beginning to sag because of the amount of water held by the paper trash in the back of the truck. It soaked up the rain and made the trash many times it's dry weight. "Dump closes at three and I reckon we is getting close. And if we load her up too much, we will bust the truck again."

The sky was beginning to lighten up already, and the rain had slowed to a steady shower. The lightning had moved on to the east. Stinky climbed out of the truck and went around to the passenger side laid down on the ground and slid under the truck to wiggle the wires on the starter. It was easy to slide under with the coating of ice marbles on the ground.

Jonas was studying something moving in the tree across Sophia in the Thomas's yard. "They's sumpin' in that tree ain't there

Ma?" Jonas was getting suspicious "Maybe it's a squirrel. Maybe a 'coon. Is 'coons in town?" Jonas answered his own question. "No coons ain't in town."

"It's a cat." Dora looked where Jonas was pointing.

Stinky pulled himself out from under the truck and started to get up just as Jonas kicked open the door to the truck. The door flew open hitting Stinky in the back and projecting him across the narrow gap between the truck and the railing above the drainage ditch. The oil on his boots, the water, and the hail all conspired to send his feet over the edge and under the pipe guardrail. The ditch was ten feet wide and eight feet deep and drained the entire north-west side of town. The downpour had filled it to near capacity and soon as Stinky's feet hit the water it yanked him under the railing and into the huge culvert under the street.

"Where'd he go Ma?" Jonas had caught glimpse of Stinky ""He jumped in the water Ma. Didja see him Ma? He threwed hisself in the water." Jonas jumped out of the truck and stood staring down into the water directly below the railing. Stinky was already half a block down Sophia, but Jonas was waiting for him to come up right where he had fallen in. The rain had nearly stopped and Dora scooted over into the driver's seat and was looking down the ditch intently.

"Get in the truck Jonas." Dora started the truck.

"What about the kitty?" Jonas was looking worriedly toward the tree across the street.

"It run off. Get in the truck." Dora was looking down the ditch to the north, watching Stinky's head bob up and down in the current.

Dora wasn't too worried. She knew Stinky could swim. "Get in the truck boy."

"You sure 'bout that cat Ma. I don' wanna leave no cat stuck in the tree." Jonas was looking doubtfully at the tree. "Poor kitty might need me."

"Get in the truck boy." Dora started up the truck and took off north down Sophia following the route of the drainage ditch. They got down to the corner of Sophia and Sycamore just in time to see Stinky grab onto a pipe that ran across the ditch. The pipe would normally be seven feet above the bottom of the ditch but was just about a foot above water level now. He grabbed on and wrapped his arms around the pipe. His boots tugged hard for a moment and then both of them pulled off. His pants started pulling down next but he was afraid to let go to hold on to them. His outer pair of pants pulled down around his knees, then Stinky kicked them the rest of the way off. His inside pants had a better piece of twine on them and so stayed put. He was thinking about working his way over to the edge of the ditch when a big tree branch bobbed up about two feet away and speared him end-on, right in the ribs. It knocked his breath out and he dropped off the pipe back into the water.

Dora had gotten up almost alongside Stinky when the branch knocked him loose. That stick was Stinky's downfall, but also his salvation. He grabbed onto it to keep himself afloat. Dora revved up the truck and roared down Grove Street toward where the ditch came out on Walnut. She caught sight of Stinky as he bobbed toward the under pass at Baker. The water from south Baker flowed into the big ditch at this point and crashed Stinky into the north side of the underpass, beating him against the limestone walls. Dora headed north on Baker then west on the alley between Oak and

Walnut, running the stop sign at Oak street in her hurry. They traveled this alley twice a week picking up trash and she knew there was a low water bridge where the water spread out and slowed down before it's last quick rush out to Spring River. She bounced the truck down the alley splashing mud everywhere and obscuring the windshield. The rain was slow now but the wiper was working very erratically and so just spread the mud out. Dora crashed across the alley running north and south and slammed on the brakes and nothing happened. The truck just barely slowed down. She pumped frantically with no results so as a last resort she gave it the gas and hoped to run clear through the low water bridge and out the other side before the water washed the truck away.

"Ma! Slow down Ma! Stop Ma! Don't try ta jump it Ma! We won't never make it Ma." Jonas was frantically begging "Oh Ma!"

Stinky popped into view on their left just as the front wheels of the truck hit the water. A huge wave rolled up from the front of the truck as it barreled through the water, three foot deep and ten or twelve feet wide. The wave caught Stinky and rolled him west out of the ditch and into a quiet back water, along the south west side of the low water bridge. The truck crashed through the water and bounced up the west side of the water throwing nearly every piece of trash out of the back and bouncing Dora and Jonas nearly to pieces in the process. Dora pumped wildly at the brakes again to get them to catch to prevent them from rolling backwards back into the water. Much to her relief the brakes held. She turned the key off to the truck and put it in gear (it had bounced out of gear and killed the engine when they hit the water) to make sure it stayed put and jumped out to check on Stinky.

"Elroy you lost your boots." Dora was watching as Stinky waded out of the water. "That's the second pair today."

"Pa didya' see it Pa. We jumped the water. Ma roared into the water and we jumped 'er." Jonas was looking at the truck with admiration. "She looks right nice all washed off don't she Pa. I didn't know this'er truck could jump water. Did ya see it? You loose another pair o' boots Pa?"

"Get in the truck boy" Stinky needed to sit down. "Did ya drown the truck Dora?"

"The brakes wasn't a workin' sos I gunned 'er through the water. I din't wannna be stopin in the water."

Stinky climbed into the truck leaned his head back against the back glass and rested a couple of minutes, then turned the key on, stepped on the starter pedal and the truck lurched forward. He put his foot on the brake pedal and yanked the truck out of gear then stabbed his foot down on the starter pedal. The truck began to roll backwards toward the water.

"We is goin backards Pa! Is we goin backards through the water Pa? Can this 'ere truck fly over the water backards? I don't wanna do it again Pa." Jonas began to frantically tug at the door handle preparatory to jumping out but the door wouldn't open so he started rolling the window down to leap out that way.

Stinky double-pedaled the starter, heel of his bare foot on the gas, toe on the starter pedal. The truck was beginning to roll into the swirling water when it fired off with a bang and Stinky yanked it into gear and lunged forward away from the flood. He drove along slowly in first gear with his foot on the brake and in just a few yards they began to grab and the right front wheel would lock up.

"Reckon the brakes was wet." Stinky drove the truck up the hill and turned left to go back to Oak Street. The western sky was beginning to clear and the sun was shining in under them, making everything stand out in sharp relief against the black angry clouds in the east. Stinky pumped the brakes some more to make sure they were working as he pulled the truck up to Baker Blvd. The brakes seemed OK now. He turned the truck right and went down to Chestnut and headed east, back toward Marvin's office. Trash cans, tree limbs, leaves, trash, clothing still clipped on the line strung out in the street, wires off the electric poles all around, no longer sparking and flashing like they did when they first fell. As the truck topped the first hill on Chestnut, Stinky saw Monty Montgomery's truck parked in front of Wollford's house. Monty was standing and studying the arrangement of the anvil and Stinky's boots.

Stinky pulled the truck over, parked, and climbed out. "You want my anvil?" Stinky was limping and hopping across the street hurting his feet on the refuse blown everywhere.

"She looks OK to me Stinky. How much you want fer it?" Monty had looked the anvil over and had even found that the hardy hole and the pritchel hole and horn were fine. There were even some hardys laying alongside and were in good condition.

"Gimme a offer." Stinky put on his trading hat. He wasn't determined not to do like Morely Wofford always did and set a price, that he found out later, was too low.

"Stinky I'll give ya thirty dollars, but it'll cost ya ten to get yer boots back." Monty figured the anvil would cost him a hundred without the hardys. They were worth about fifteen each and it was a nice size anvil. He could mount it for use with bigger work.

"I'll take the thirty, keep the boots." Stinky held out his hand in anticipation.

"I ain't got thirty dollars on me Stinky. You'll have to come round to the shop and I'll pay you." Monty leaned down and tested the weight of the anvil.

"Fer a dollar I'll help yer load it." Stinky knew what the anvil weighed.

"I'll keep my dollar Stinky." Monty squatted down, reached around the ends of the anvil and rocked it back and forth. With a mighty lift he picked it up and set it on his thighs while he was still squatting. Then with a controlled ease he stood up and walked to the back of his truck. Stinky was so surprised he could hardly believe his eyes. Monty set the anvil down on the truck and it sank noticeably. "Bout a two hunerd fifty or three hunnert pound I'd say."

Stinky watched in wonder as Monty picked up the hardys and tossed them in the floor of his truck.

Stinky began to shuffle back to his truck avoiding the larger obstacles."I'll come over for my money later."

"Stinky! Here's your boots." Monty carried Stinky's boots carefully him. They were both nearly full of water. Monty was considering Stinky. Stinky really looked bad. Roughed up and wet clear through. More holes in his clothes than usual. Tired looking.

156

"I ain't gonna pay ten dollars fer em. You better keep em." Stinky continued across the street.

"No Elroy, I don't want your money. I was just joshin' ya. Here's your boots." Monty poured the water out of the boots as he crossed the road, shook them out, and handed them to Stinky.

"Much 'bliged" Stinky gratefully pulled on the boots, pulled the right one back off, rubbed some chat off the bottom of his foot, and put it back on. "Much 'bliged."

"You come for your money when you get home." Monty watched as Stinky stumbled back to his truck. "You OK Stinky?"

Stinky just waved and went on back to the truck and climbed in. Dora had gotten a cigarette lit somehow and was puffing happily. Jonas had gotten out of the foul smoke in the cab and had found his comic under the seat, miraculously dry. He was standing in the sunshine in the back of the truck leafing through to find his spot, the dark storm clouds all moving on to the east.

Stinky drove up Chestnut then turned right at Clinton and went up two blocks to Marvin McDonald's house. Stinky knew, since Marvin's car was there, he was probably home.

Marvin saw Stinky drive up and hustled to get his ledger and get outside so Stinky wouldn't be tempted to come in his house. "Howdy Stinky. You done on your route?" Marvin wasn't really interested but he had some uncomfortable news to give to Stinky.

"Storm messed it up. Blew trash everwheres." Stinky was worried about the way Marvin was looking at him.

"That's fine Stinky. You ain't gotta pick none of it what isn't in cans." Marvin was thinking of other things.

There was a long pause while Marvin studied his ledger to make sure he hadn't made a mistake or that the city clerk hadn't. "Stinky I got sumpin' to tell you about your pay."

Marvin looked uncomfortable and Stinky feared the worst "I know we was slow today, you can dock us if yous got to. I unerstan'." Stinky stood staring at his boots. The toes of both boots were now rather flat and it made them fit better.

"It ain't that." Marvin couldn't bring himself to say it.

"If it's about selling that anvil, I ain't got no money for it yet." Stinky hoped Marvin wasn't going to take away his salvage right to the trash he picked up.

"Anvil? No it ain't about an anvil." Marvin screwed himself up and just said it. "I gotta pay you eight dollars more for every week you picked up trash for me."

Stinky just stood there thinking. He had picked up trash for nearly seven years now for Marvin. He had done the work since he was fourteen, but just seven years for Marvin.

"I gotta give you seven hunerd and twenty eight dollars extra, every week for the next four weeks. Less tax and Social Security of course." Marvin could hear himself say it, but could hardly believe it. Marvin had been told that paying Stinky and the accompanying Social Security tax as well as his own, would probably keep him out of jail. The city attorney had been very clear that if he did not pay, he would be visiting the county lock-up.

"Why you gonna give me this money Marvin? I don't want it lessn it's mine." Stinky was very suspicious of Marvin giving away anything. He squeezed pennies so hard Mr. Lincoln complained.

"It is yours Stinky. The city clerk says I done my books wrong and I gotta pay you. Here's your check." Marvin handed him the check.

Stinky just stared at it. It was more money than he had ever had in his life at one time. "Much 'bliged."

"You're welcome." Marvin almost felt like Stinky deserved it, the way he looked today.

Stinky went back to the truck and climbed in. He didn't know quite what to say. So, he didn't say anything. He just sat there.

"Whatchoo doin Elroy?" Ma looked at him suspiciously. "Did you let that Marvin talk you in to puttin' off your pay?"

Stinky thought about that, "No Ma. I gots my pay."

"Well you better." Ma looked belligerently at Marvin's house, her suspicions well based, but not confirmed.

"Reckon we best go to Albert's store to pick up whatever it was he wanted us to haul." Stinky started the truck and drove around the block and back over to the Chestnut where he turned west, then back north on Garrison and back to Winston's Market. They reached the store without incident and Monty pulled around back of the store.

Stinky climbed out of the truck and went into the store by the back way. Albert Wright was alone in the store and he jumped up to show Stinky the special load of trash. He was prepared to hustle

Stinky out of the store, when he realized he couldn't smell him. "My nose must have quit working." He thought to himself. Then he realized Stinky looked like he had been very wet.

"Howdy Stinky. Quite a storm huh?" Albert was chatty out of habit, "Guess you got caught out in it." He looked Stinky's still very damp figure over.

"Yeah. Wet." Stinky agreed.

"Well here it is. This is out-of-date canned and boxed goods. See the one's with the red exs on 'em? Soup, beans, canned vegetables, tomaters, applesauce, rice, macaroni. It's all out of date and the grocery supplier says he don't wanta haul it back, so he paid me to hire someone to haul it away. You want the job?" Albert saw the boxes as trash, Stinky saw it as months, worth of food. Albert went on,"I'll pay you two dollars."

Stinky was shocked. He was prepaired to pay Albert for the boxes of food, then it struck him that this was just another trash pick-up to Albert.

"Two dollars and a pack of Camels and a box o' crackerjack." Stinky decided he could afford to bargain, even on a deal like this.

"You got a deal. Let me help load it up." Albert grabbed the top case of macaroni and headed out the door.

"Jonas! Come help carry this stuff." Stinky was looking at the neat stack of food boxes with red wax pencil marks on them all.

"Is all this trash Pa? It don't look like trash Pa. Is you sure it's trash Pa? Is we gonna throw it all away Pa?" Jonas had climbed out, and trotted over to join Stinky, his just about bugging out. "Trucks ain't gonna run over this like them donuts, is they?"

"Just load up the ones with red x's on them boy." Stinky, Jonas and Albert made four trips each, carrying the boxes, and then Jonas finished up while Albert and Stinky finished their trade.

"Come on back in and I'll Pay you Elroy." Albert was feeling like he had gotten a bargain. The wholesale grocery distributor charged Albert a percentage to haul off out-of-date food. If Albert threw away the out-of-date products himself, he and the grocery distributor representative counted and marked all the food as they packed it up in boxes, then Albert got full credit for the old product. Albert figured the deal with Stinky was good. "Here's the cigarettes, and the Crackerjacks and the two dollars, and here take a chocolate to the misses."

"Much 'bliged" Stinky collected his treasures and headed out.

"Jonas here's you sumpin'." Stinky tossed Jonas the crackerjack. "Dora, here." He handed Dora the cigarettes, started to give her the chocolate, then unwrapped it and ate it himself. Dora would rather have her cigarettes.

"Elroy I ain't 'sposed to buy ready rolled cigarettes. They costs too much." Dora was looking reproachfully at Stinky.

"Keep em. Today's payday." Stinky was thinking of the check in his pocket and the food in the back of the truck. He started the truck and headed for home. As they pulled up in front of his house he saw smoke coming from the chimney and fat Leopold's car was there.

"Jonas you get Leopold and carry all this food in the house. I gotta go see Monty." Stinky climbed out of the truck and started down the street.

"Pa you want some coffee" Marcia was looking out the front door of the house "It be fresh brewed from the coffee you brung home."

"Yeah. Black." Stinky waited a moment and Leopold lumbered out to begin carrying all the discarded food into the house. He was followed by Jonas, and shortly, by Marcia, with his coffee. "Much 'bliged."

Stinky had one more errand before his day was up. He walked around the corner to Monty's shop and found the big doors were closed but the little one was open and the light of the lantern shown inside.

Monty was sitting at his desk, the anvil Stinky had sold him was sitting on a big, blackened, red oak stump that had spent countless years in the back corner of Monty's shop, waiting for an anvil, an anvil that Monty had just never had the spare cash to buy.

"I got your money here Stinky." Monty stood up and carried it to the door where Stinky stood. Stinky's outline looked rough, kind of banged up and ragged.

"Much 'bliged." Stinky started to turn away then stopped. "Coffee ya give us is right good." he saluted Monty with the cup.

That gave Monty a start. "You all right Elroy? You look like you had a hard day." He was feeling a little guilty about that coffee.

"Oh it wasn't bad. I'd say 'bout average." Stinky answered and he turned for home.

The big compacting garbage trucks and hired haulers took some of the "charm" away from trash hauling, and Mrs. Courtney was enraged at the fact that now she paid for her trash pickup at the same time that she paid for her exorbitant water, sewer and electric. The new trash men didn't take the stuff she threw away in payment like Stinky Randall. A coat the neighbors dog had been using for a bed in his dog house had been worth a week's trash pickup to Stinky. The Randalls noticed the dog hair on the coat but they never noticed the smell. When the new trucks rolled in, Mrs. Courtney tried trading a kerosene iron that had caught fire, for her first week's trash pickup. The boys on the truck were rude. She assumed they just didn't know her and understand the way she did business. She was wrong. They understood all too well.

Church on Sunday, when it was good weather, was a part of Mrs. Courtney's regular schedule. She went to Fourth Street Baptist Church. They had church only on Sundays and then only in the morning. No Sunday night service, no mid- week service. No full time minister. No heavy doctrine. No guilt laid on the church members. Mild mannered and often backward young men, frightened nearly to death of speaking in front of a crowd, and often not well schooled, kept themselves to well trod non-controversial scripture. Mrs. Courtney read her bible. Believed it all, and practiced what her father and mother had taught her. "God takes care of those who take care of themselves." Her church never interfered with this premise until one Sunday in 1962 the Rev. J.L Lincoln was assigned to preach at Fourth Street Baptist. J. L. was mistakenly assigned to Fourth Street Baptist on the first Sunday in August. A young man named Samuel Johnson was sent to the all *black Second Street Baptist Church. It was educational for all involved.*

The Awakening

Johnny Peters carefully parked his nearly new, pale green, 1962 Mercury two-door in the spot next to the "reserved for visiting preacher" spot, right where he always parked at Fourth Street Baptist Church. He studied the gauges on the car's dash, noting that the oil pressure and engine temperature were good, but the voltage perhaps a tad low. "Maybe he should change the generator brushes or clean the battery terminals." He thought, then went on, working his way through possibilities for the low voltage, until his train of thought was interrupted by his wife Melinda.

"Well are you gonna' sit here in a brown study all mornin'?" She said crossly, "It's hot as hades in here, and my hind end is sticking to these plastic seat covers you put on."

"Gotta keep the upholstery clean. It improves the resale value." Johnny patted the steering wheel, and Melinda snorted, knowing that Johnny would probably be buried with this car. "Besides, I'm just checking the gauges."

They could hear the big courthouse clock chiming as Johnny shut the car off, with a little blip of the throttle just to hear the twin pipes pop, right on the stroke of nine AM.

Most Sundays, they were the first arrivals, carrying out their duty to open up the Fourth Street Baptist Church for Sunday morning service. Johnny was the Sunday School Superintendent, and he took his responsibilities seriously. He was also the chairman of the building maintenance committee, and the Adult Sunday School teacher. Melinda played the organ and liked to practice before Sunday School started, and Johnny always needed to look up the opening scripture and read it through.

He swung his legs out of the big Mercury and strode purposely to the building, his boots crunching in the chat parking lot. He unlocked the right-hand door on the northwest corner of the building, and swung open half of the ornate, round-topped, teak door, and the stale air, building up in the church all week, boiled out. The doors, a gift from some long ago church attendee, were the only decorative part of the building. The remainder was pure function. The left hand door had stuck shut at some time in the dim history, and Johnny had never seen it open.

Melinda stepped into the church commenting as the heat struck her, "Maybe the idea of calling off church in August is not so bad." She picked up one of the "Jesus in the Garden" cardboard fans with the tongue depressor handle (Courtesy of the Lenk's Funeral Home L. Lenk proprietor.) and began to fan herself, the white ribbon on her pale pink Sunday hat flapping in the breeze she created.

Johnny began to systematically open the big windows down the south side of the sanctuary, cursing under his breath at the ones with the counterweights missing, fumbling with the sticks to wedge them up, while precariously holding them up with the other hand.

"Wish we could to get someone that owns an air conditioning shop to start coming to church here. Hell. Maybe just someone that owns a hardware store that sells them window units." Johnny switched to the north side of the room searching for the stick for the west window and finally finding it tucked into the cushion on the second row pew. "'Course them window units take two twenty and we just barely got one ten in this place."

Melinda plugged in the little fan behind the organ and poked at the brass fan blade with a pencil, until it began to turn. She had, when the fan first quit starting up right, poked at it with her fingers. It surprised her one morning by starting right up and gave her fingers a thumping. She mournfully told Johnny it had affected her playing something awful, and had been insulted when he had commented that he "hadn't noticed any difference at all". She aimed the little fan so it blew on her legs while she sat on the organ bench, hiking her dress up a bit to get the cooling breeze in underneath.

"It would be nice just to have a fan that started without me risking my fingers to get it to run." She began pumping the foot pedals and held one key down till the old organ wheezed into action. "I think it's leaking again."

Johnny stopped opening windows to listen. "The tape must have come off."

"Well I am not crawling around on my knees in my new stockings to patch that old bellows again. They can just listen to the leak till someone decides to pay to have it fixed." Melinda pounded out a few chords to emphasize her feelings. "I could go down to First Baptist and play their big fancy pipe organ if I wanted. I was invited to you know."

"Yes dear I know." He answered clearly; then continued by muttering, "You've told me many times. Many, many, many, many, many times." Johnny's voice rose so Melinda almost heard the last words, but not quite.

Johnny went to the front of the church and entered the little hallway between the sanctuary and the fellowship hall. He picked up a wooden broomstick, reached way up high above the doorway to the baptistery and pushed the big knife switch up. The big open switch ran the motor to the ceiling fans. The motor was way up in the peak of the building, in line with the fans, which were out in the sanctuary, suspended at least twenty feet in the air. There was a pair of flat leather belts that ran through a little opening in the wall and out to the fans. The belts squeaked loudly when the motor was first switched on, and then calmed down into a soothing rhythm of little sighs and squeaks and clicks as the big wooden-bladed fans got up to speed. Johnny had spent untold Sundays listening to the belts and the little sounds they made. Swish, swish, swish, click, swish, swish, swish and the muffled click as the belt went over the motor pulley back behind the wall. It was fun to anticipate the "click" as the steel staples that held the ends of the belts together touched the pulleys. He had, once, almost worked out how many miles those little clips traveled during an ordinary Sunday sermon, when his mental math page had been erased by the premature ending of the sermon. It was the only time Johnny could remember being annoyed by a preacher ending his diatribe early.

He retrieved his Bible from the drawer of the table in the foyer, where he left it each week. For years he had carried his Bible home each Sunday, but he forgot to bring it back quite often, so he began leaving it at the church. He had no use for it during the week anyway. He went back to the sanctuary and took up his regular seat

168

in the second row and looked up this weeks opening scripture all the time keeping an eye out for the arrival of a stranger who would more than likely turn out to be this weeks preacher.

Almost every week the Southern Baptist Administration found a "preacher" to send to Forth Street Baptist Church. Fourth Street could never have afforded a full time minister on the offerings, and the last part-time man had quit, after finding out what his wages were.

So, every week a stranger would come and feed the congregation from the word of God, and then disappear back to wherever he had come from, never to be seen again.

Johnny and Melinda had been gone to see their new grand-baby one weekend. (Johnny had actually gone fishing that Sunday with his boy, but that wasn't anyone's business.) Ed Morse was the assistant Sunday School superintendent and had taken Johnny's place at church that morning. Ed had badly confused a poor vagrant that had wandered into the church, by assuming that the poor man was the preacher the Association had sent to them that week. In Ed's defense the vagrant was dressed at least as well as some of the preachers they had been sent.

"Who is preaching this week?" Melinda shouted over the organ's groaning.

"Schedule says somebody named J.L. Lincoln. He was assigned by the Southern Baptist Administrator. He ain't even a regular circuit preacher." Johnny had lost his place in his Bible looking for the note with the preacher's name and was busily thumbing for Matthew. "He couldn't help but be an improvement over last week." He finally gave up searching and went to the index.

Johnny hoped this preacher was old enough to have outgrown the squeak in his voice and the acne. The speaker the previous Sunday had been terrible. His name had been Dewey. Reverend Dewey used words Johnny had never heard before. Johnny and Melinda had discussed some of the words on the way home, debating whether Dewey had been given a thesaurus and tried to use it, or had just made the words up. Johnny thought the latter. "I tell you I ain't never heard no-body say fabrigalted or misbespeckled before."

Abruptly the wheezing of the organ stopped and Johnny glanced at his watch. Half passed nine.

The choir was scheduled to sing, and Amanda Adams was the first member to arrive. "Morning Johnny!" She squeaked as she passed him on her way to the choir robe closets up by the baptistery, her high heels beating a rapid tattoo on the hardwood floor.

"Morning Mel!" she intoned as she passed the organ where Melinda was organizing her music.

"Morning Amanda." Melinda answered, wincing at her name being shortened to "Mel". Somehow it sounded like a man's name when Amanda did that.

Amanda went straight to work, pulling out the black choir notebooks and checking that they all had the right music in them. Amanda had once been confounded by the men in the choir, when all three of them had begun a different song than the ladies. That was not going to happen again!

LouElla Courtney showed up shortly after Melinda, pulled open the robe closet and picked through them to find her own favorite. "Who is coming to choir today Amanda?" she asked, as she prepared to count out the robes.

"All the ladies, and Harold and Hubert." Amanda answered while yanking a few pages out of a music notebook and re-inserting them in the correct order and orientation.

"Well I hope Hubert stays awake." LouElla had pulled out her lint brush and was working on one of the larger robes. "I wish he would get him some of that blue stuff."

"Blue stuff?" Amanda stopped sorting pages, wondering what LouElla was talking about.

"You know," LouElla replied, giving the robe shoulders a few more violent scrubs with the lint brush, "that blue stuff for scabies or lice or whatever it is."

"It's not scabies LouElla, and it certainly isn't lice. It's itchy scalp and flakes." Amanda was scandalized, "Poor Hubert can't help it."

"Well, maybe not, I just hope if he sleeps, he doesn't snore this time." LouElla scowled at the thought, scrubbing even more ferociously on the shoulders,

"He's such a nice boy." Amanda swooned a little "Sooo nice."

"Hurumph." LouElla considered Amanda's words, and found them wanting, "He's thirty-four years old, pudgy, and pale as paste, and he lives with his mother."

"Now LouElla you know he takes such good care of Eunice." Eunice Clay was Hubert's mother and a soprano in the choir.

171

"His momma should be ashamed for keeping him tied to her apron strings." LouElla abruptly changed tack, "We do need a tenor in choir though. Even if he does have dandruff."

They wrapped up their tasks just as Johnny dinged the little bell, indicating the start of Sunday school.

Sunday school was in the fellowship hall, and very informal at the Fourth Street Baptist Church. In the winter there was hot coffee and hot tea. In the summer, hot coffee and iced tea, (sweetened or unsweetened, with creamer or without) and every fifth Sunday, there were doughnuts. The tea and coffee were courtesy of Midge's Diner and big Ed Morse (owner, cook, waiter, bus boy and cashier). He made sure there were drinks for all. He only charged a little over what it cost him, and the Southern Baptist Association was none the wiser. He always took what was left over, back to the diner. "Waste not. Want not." was his motto. All appreciated Ed's sacrifice.

The doughnuts came from Enos Mack up at the L&M Restaurant. He gave them the leftovers from Saturday, since they were closed fifth Sundays and by Monday the doughnuts would be too old to be good.

There were sliding partitions for different classes back in the fellowship hall, and if you were bored with your own teacher, you could listen to one of the others. There would only be three classes today: Young marrieds, Adults, and Patriarchs. The joke, though not very humorous, was that there were no men in the Patriarch class. There hadn't been a promotion Sunday since Alice Stokes' grandson had quit coming to church ten years before. ("Grandma, do I have to go to that class with Mrs. Beal? She smells so awful, and she has a mustache.") There were no children's classes now,

(Henrietta Beal had passed away) so there were no promotions from Young Adults as long as Hubert remained a bachelor, to push the Young Marrieds on into the Adult class. Now the Young Marrieds were mostly in their fifties and sixties and the ladies only moved on to the Patriarch class when their husbands died. There used to be, when Johnny and Melinda's kids had been little, children in the church, but that was twenty years gone and there were no youngsters in the church now.

Twenty-seven people attended Sunday School on this particular morning and Melinda had moved to the piano in the fellowship hall and was warming up the keys. She had difficulties with the transition from the pump organ to piano, which could be attested to by the scrapes on the lower front of the piano, resulting from Melinda forgetting and peddling her feet when she wanted the piano louder. There was also something about the immediacy of the sound that came out of the piano that threw off her timing and it made for interesting rhythms to the choruses they sang to start the opening ceremony.

People worked their way in as Johnny sat at the back and re-read his short list of things they needed to talk about in the pre-class assembly. Ed Morse showed up and put together the big coffee maker and started it perking. Amanda and LouElla had moved from choir robes to tea preparation and had been joined by half a dozen other women as the morning progressed. Soon a small group had gathered, most holding big white mugs and catching up with each other on what had happened in town during the week.

"Psst" Melinda looked at her watch and hissed at Johnny. "Psst....Johnny!"

Johnny stopped stirring his coffee and looked around, aware something was going on but not sure what. He had been studying a lump of something swirling around with the creamer in his big porcelain mug, trying to decide if it was coffee grounds, or a bug.

Melinda played piano with her left hand and tapped her watch with her right as Johnny stared blankly at her. Then he jumped and looked at his own watch and then regretfully set down his cup of coffee and walked up to the podium in the front of the fellowship hall, reached down inside and turned on the sound system. After an appropriate amount of time for the tubes to warm up, Johnny tried a timid "Hello?"

As usual, someone had messed with the knobs and no sound came out. Johnny twisted the volume knob, realized the switch on the microphone was off and flipped it on. The immediate result got everyone's attention, as the amplifier screamed with feedback until Johnny got the volume turned back down.

"Why in the world do you turn that thing on?" Fred Long said crossly from the back of the hall, as he tried to wipe the coffee off his good dress pants. "You scare us to death with that racket and there's only twenty of us here. We can hear you for God's sake."

"Twenty seven." George Mason corrected Fred. He had just counted and put the numbers up on the hymn board in the sanctuary. "It's a good thing there ain't just twenty people here, cause I ain't got enough zeros to make a twenty. I need more zeros and twos."

Everyone just ignored George. He was always going on about not having enough zeros and twos for the hymn board. Johnny had once suggested that George just use a one instead of a zero and

George was mad at him for weeks. George still wasn't sure he trusted Johnny after that kind of crooked suggestion.

"Stand for the opening chorus." Johnny picked up the dog-eared little paperback chorus book Choice Songs and opened it to the marked page, "Turn to page thirty two."

"Thirty one" Melinda hissed at Johnny.

"Oh....thirty one." Johnny corrected himself.

Melinda pounded out the last few measures of the song as an introduction, and Johnny searched in his mind for the first note, not really sure what key she was in. "Father in Heaven, Hear us today." He wandered across the spectrum of notes until finally reaching approximately the same key Melinda was playing in. "Hallowed Thy name be; Hear us we pray!" Just then it occurred to Johnny that the microphone was still turned on, and he reached up and turned it off with a loud thump, as if a bass drum had been added for emphasis. That surprised some of the congregation and "O let thy Kingdom come, O let thy will be done," was barely audible above the piano, but with Melinda leading the way and pounding in a couple of measures (in a different time signature) that weren't in the song before the final phrase, there was a grand finale worthy of any group of Baptists "By all beneath the sun, as in the skies." Not for the first time, Johnny wondered what in the world that last phrase meant. He had tried to ask Melinda once, but she had acted flabbergasted and he had dropped the subject.

As the song ended, Elgin Eds stood and began to clear his throat (like he always did before he spoke) but much to everyone's surprise Willis Young stood at the same time, his eyes squeezed shut and a death grip on the wooden chair in front of him, and he began to pray, "Our Father", The chair vibrated under Willis's hands and the leg with the missing rubber cap beat a little tattoo on the concrete floor. "I pray for guidance in the time of trouble." At this point half the little group quit listening. They knew the rest of his prayer by heart. Elgin Eds cleared his throat even more vigorously still determined to have his proper turn at the morning prayer, until his wife Cynthia gave him a stiff elbow to the ribs and the throat clearing turned into an "Ooooofffff" and then silence.

"I pray for peace for all at war. I ask for guidance for our government, and strength to carry out your will in all things. Amen"

Everyone intoned "Amen", but anyone near where the Eds sat, heard Elgin's stage whisper to Cynthia, "But it was my turn."

"George?" Johnny forgot to turn the microphone back on, thought a moment and then just spoke up louder, not wanting to repeat the previous debacle. "George! Do you have a report for us?"

George Mason stood, shuffling a hand full of papers, and dropping some of the numbers that he had exchanged for different ones on the hymn board this morning. "Give me a moment Mr. Chairman." confusing Johnny, who was Superintendent of Sunday School with Elgin Eds who was in fact the chairman of the deacons. "Oh....Here we are. Argh...arumph....humpf..." He took a quick sip of his coffee to clear his throat, choked on it a bit which in turn caused him to drop more numbers, including one zero, which he had believed had been stolen by vandals. "Oh! There you are!" He picked the zero up and showed it to the little group who, being accustomed to his vagaries were mostly ignoring him. "I found another zero!" he announced happily. Staring at it like the father had looked upon his prodigal son upon his return.

Johnny checked his watch, "George? Do you have a report."

"Oh! Yes Mr. Chairman." George again started sorting through items stuffed in his Bible for safekeeping making everyone fear a repeat of what had just happened. "Where are you? You little devil. Oh! Here we go." George smiled broadly and began to haltingly read, "Forty three, Twenty seven, zero, one hundred sixty two, "

"George!" Johnny interrupted him, "Tell us what each number is for."

"Oh! OK." George answered as if this request had never been made before, when in fact he had to be reminded almost every Sunday. "Forty three people. Twenty six people."

"George!" Johnny's patience was being put to the test today. "Tell us what days."

"Well, it's always Sundays Johnny, unless it is Wednesday, but Wednesday is always zero now, since we quit having a prayer meeting, which is why I am always low on zeros." George shuffled through his papers and held up his card with the zero on it to illustrate.

"George, now listen." Johnny decided to get at it the hard way. "George, how many people in Sunday School last week?"

"Let me see." George began shuffling papers again, "Where did you go you little devil you?"

"George." Johnny tried to keep the exasperation out of his voice, "Look in your left hand, under your Bible."

"There you are!" George was genuinely pleased and smiled pleasantly at Johnny.

"Well?"

"Well what Johnny?"

"How many people in Sunday School last Sunday?" Johnny could feel the corner of his eye beginning to twitch.

"Well, let's see." George squinted at the paper. "Twenty six."

"How many this week?"

"Twenty seven" George looked at Johnny and continued, "I thought you would remember that Johnny, I already told you."

Johnny ignored his reprimand and went on, "How many folks were at Church last week George?"

"Well, If you add Sunday School and Church together you get sixty nine, so that is how many was at Church, but some of them are the same people, so it don't really count."

"It's OK George. Just tell us what the offering was last week." Johnny thought that would perk up the sleepers, and he was right.

"Well, it wasn't good Johnny." George looked suitably sad "It was eighty three dollars and eighty eight cents. If Arnold hadn't turned eighty eight and brung eighty eight pennies for his birthday offering, we would have just got eighty three dollars."

Johnny knew it wasn't good. He knew what needed fixed on the building better than anyone. He also knew there was no money in the budget to fix anything.

178

"Anything else Mr. Chair, uh....Johnny?" George was carefully packing all his papers into his bible.

"No George. Thank you very much." Johnny was still on the lookout for the new preacher, looking back through the hallway and in toward the front doors. "We will sing our separation song now."

Melinda began pounding out a tune, but Johnny was completely mystified as to what it was when thankfully, Amanda Adams began "God be with you 'till we meet again."

The congregation joined in at this point, "By his counsel's guide, uphold you." There was another of those lines to a song that Johnny found baffling, but had learned to ignore.

"With his sheep securely fold you." Johnny always figured the feller that wrote the song must not of ever been around sheep, or he wouldn't have thought it was nice to be folded up with one.

"God be with you till we meet again." The congregation finished strong as a few of the members stood and made their way over to their side of the fellowship hall, and the widows trouped en-masse back to the sanctuary where they met for the Patriarch class.

Hubert Clay arrived just in time to help roll out the center divider. The process went smoothly until he reached a crack in the floor that grabbed the front edge of the partition and yanked it out of his hands.

Johnny watched in fascination at this little act being played out, almost unbelieving that Hubert could do this every Sunday. But he did. Hubert stood there looking surprised as the partition folded its self back into its little cubby. Hubert's mother, Eunice, watched with pride as her Hubert marched purposefully after the escaping wall and wrestled it into submission, dragging it across the room and over that pesky crack in the floor, then pushing the latching mechanism together, over and over and over, until it finally meshed just right, and clicked into place.

Johnny relinquished the little bell to Hubert, who dutifully dinged the little bell into the microphone, (which was still turned off) and then Hubert left, to go sit with his mother in the Patriarch, class until time to ding the little bell again, signifying the end of Sunday School.

"Good morning" Johnny said as he stepped over to the "Young Marrieds" side of the fellowship hall.

"'Morning Johnny" the little group responded.

"Mitch, can you read," Johnny stopped here and consulted a lesson plan page from his Bible, "Mathew fourteen fifteen through twenty-one?" Johnny knew this group well, and knew just who to call on to read the scripture. When some of the folks in this group read the scripture, it turned into a drone, like an airplane out in the distance, and others mangled the words so badly it was hard to tell what scripture they were reading. Mitch was one of the safe ones.

"Sure Johnny. Let me look that up." Mitchell Shore was the closest thing to a scholar that attended Forth Street Baptist, but he was shy and would never actually teach. He would, as Johnny knew, read the passage asked for, and rarely botch it up. "Here we are. And when it was evening, his disciples came to him, saying, This is a desert place, and the time is now past; send the multitude away, that they may go into the villages, and buy themselves victuals. But Jesus said unto them, They need not depart; give ye them to eat. And they say unto him, We have here but five loaves, and two fishes. He said, bring them hither to me. And he commanded the multitude to sit down on the grass, and took the five loaves, and the two fishes, and looking up to heaven, he blessed, and brake, and gave the loaves to his disciples, and the disciples to the multitude. And they did all eat, and were filled: and they took up of the fragments that remained twelve baskets full. And they that had eaten were about five thousand men, beside women and children. There you are Johnny."

"Thank you Mitch, that was nicely done." Johnny stared at the lesson plan page again and began to read in a monotone, "A crowd of people had followed Jesus out into a desert. There was no food, except what someone had carried out in a basket. They were willing to share with Jesus and the disciples. There was not nearly enough for everyone though. Jesus was thankful for the gift from his friends and took the food and began to hand it out to others. Through this action all were fed and there was enough to fill twelve baskets when they were done. This is a testimony to how we all should be faithful and not worry when it looks like we will not have enough. Jesus will take care of us. Now have a discussion. Oh, uh not that last part, I mean, now we will look at discussion questions. The first discussion question is; What would have happened had someone not brought any food?"

There was a long painful silence and finally Elgin Eds spoke up. "I guess they all would have been hungry."

There was a little laughter at this, quickly smothered.

As usual, his wife Cynthia took the opportunity to correct him. "Why what a silly thing to say. Jesus would never let his people be hungry."

Elgin looked properly chastised and offered no rebuttal.

Another long painful silence ensued and Johnny studied the page for the next discussion question, "What lesson do we learn from the disciples wanting to send the people away to buy food, but Jesus having them stay?"

This one was tough, and the silence stretched almost unbearably before Mitch Shore spoke up. "The disciples did not understand that this was a moment when Jesus could show both power and compassion. They would have sent the people away and kept the company of Jesus to themselves, but Jesus wanted to show that all the people, even women and children should stay near him and be fed both bodily and spiritually."

"Well why wouldn't the women get to stay?" Cynthia jumped in again, more than willing to find fault with folks other than her husband as well. "And why didn't they count the women anyway? You can bet it was a woman packed that man five loaves and two fishes to go out on this hike!"

Mitch knew when to cut his losses and was silent. Anita Shores, Mitch's wife, thought about answering, but then she never spoke up in Sunday School and couldn't bring herself to do so now. She did however think unkind things about Cynthia.

At this point Johnny, confused by the disagreement, started to read the next discussion question, but was interrupted by Hubert coming in, picking up the Sunday School bell and dinging it twice into the still turned off microphone.

Johnny was relieved of the duty to try and get any more discussion started, "Well, that concludes today's Sunday School." He said quickly, "You are dismissed."

Elgin Eds spoke up. "You forgot the closing prayer!" He was still wanting his turn.

"Thank you Elgin. Would you like to have the closing prayer?"

"Yes Johnny. Thank you for asking." Elgin began to rummage through his pockets searching for his prayer notes he had prepared.

"Look in your Bible." Cynthia jumped in to save the day.

"Oh, yes. Thank you Lord for the many blessings we have each day. Thank you Lord for this place of worship that welcomes us to come and study your word. Thank you Lord for peace and prosperity in our country and for our soldiers, sailors, airplanes and marines."

"Airmen!" Cynthia hissed.

"Huh? Thank you Lord for peace and prosperity in our country and for our soldie......" Elgin lost his place as Hubert Clay released the latch on the dividing wall and it slithered back along it's track and banged into it's little alcove.

"Thank you Lord for peace and prosperity in our country and for our soldie......"

"You already said that." Cynthia was pointing at the paper trying to get him back on track.

"Oh well. Amen" Elgin gave up.

Everyone just sat there and Johnny realized they were waiting for him, so he repeated, "You are all dismissed." just as Hubert again "dinged" the little bell into the still dead microphone.

The people in Johnny's class all stood, the scooting of the wooden chairs on the concrete floor giving notice to the other classes that Sunday School had ended.

There was a general bustle as the three groups joined back up, and cups and glasses were gathered to be washed in the little kitchen in the back. Melinda rushed out to the organ and began playing her rather enthusiastic prelude music as the folks straggled out to join the few gathered in the sanctuary that had not attended Sunday School.

As it neared ten o'clock, the rest of the congregation filed in and Melinda began to play more carefully, and to her way of thinking, reverently. It was a hard transition though. Melinda was a third generation organist. Her Grandfather Leggitt had played the piano at the movie theater during silent movies and he had also played the organ at the big Methodist Church on Sundays and for funerals. Melinda's mother, Lois Platt (nee Leggitt) had followed in her father's footsteps, so to speak, but the movie house had started showing "talkies" and so Lois played at the big Methodist church until it burnt down one Monday morning during a thunderstorm, and then she switched to playing at L. Lent's Funeral Home. They had bought an electronic console organ and it was the wonder of funerals in the county. Melinda rarely went with her Momma to the funeral home, but the roller skating rink bought a second hand calliope from a defunct circus and hired Lois to play on Friday and Saturday nights. As Melinda grew up, she would occasionally play a song or two for the grade school kids skate, and eventually moved

184

into the Friday and Saturday slot, until during one of her breaks to have a baby, the roller rink bought a record player and a big horn speaker with an amplifier and sold the organ as scrap to Junior Randall. The truth was, everything Melinda played still had the touch of the roller rink to it.

She took an informal role call as people pews had been padded, but folks didn't like coming in late and not having any

Melinda missed a beat when a boy of about thirteen came in. "Kids in church?" She thought. "How inappropriate." They never knew how to act and sometimes wanted to sing strange new songs. Alice Worth followed the

"Could we......" Johnny began to speak when the choir stood and burst into song interrupting him.

"Glory and Honor, Glory and honor, Glory and Honor. AAAAAAAAAAA

"May we all listen to the words of our Lord." Johnny opened his Bible to the marked spot and began to read. "

Melinda knocked a hymnal off the organ bench and it hit the hardwood floor with a bang. Johnny glanced at her and knew it was going to be a long afternoon and life.

At Johnny's signal, Bobby Johnson stood and walked up to the microphone. He cleared his throat directly into the mic which started a ringing that took several seconds to die away. When silence again prevailed, he began to recite in a monotone, "Father bless Adam Sloat's Uncle Shad," Bobby knew if Adam's Uncle shad would quit drinking, the gout would go away, but he didn't say so,"and Please bless Norman," Here Bobby mumbled something

185

that no-one understood, and then continued, "and bless Lester Moats who needs healded."

In the choir "loft", Hubert leaned over to Harold and said in a stage whisper that could be heard to the back "I wish he'd write himself a new prayer. Thatn's wearin' a bit thin."

Harold gave Hubert an embarrassed glance and scooted away from him clamping his eyes back shut.

Bobby stuck the note back in his pocket "Also Lord guide this great country's leaders in the paths that are pleasing to you and uh..........." at this point the words choked in his throat. "Amen."

Melinda who always played background music for the prayers because it added so much to the words, was caught with several measures to go in her song. The song was written in the key of C and she let the organ wheeze down to silence on a G chord which left the congregation hanging, waiting for a resolution.

Alice Meeks stood to go to the podium to lead singing, and like every Sunday was forced to clamber out of the choir loft over Sally Yates feet. Not for the first time Johnny wondered why they didn't just trade places.

"Please turn to page sixty one in our hymnal." Alice said and stood waiting expectantly.

"That is last weeks program." Melinda hissed at Alice, shaking her head vigorously and held up the current weeks program "Us the one with the river on the front. The river!"

Alice stared at Melinda blandly and waited for her to begin the song and Melinda gave in and turned to page sixty-one and began to play.

Melinda got her way on the next song by beginning to play before Alice made the announcement of the page number and for a moment they went at cross purposes with Alice tuning to page three hundred and twenty two "Near the Cross," and Melinda playing the introduction to "How Great Thou Art." Melinda won out with the congregation joining her.

Alice got control wrestled back from Melinda on the offering song though, by breaking in before the final asthmatic note from the organ, "Now for our offering song, Be Thou My Vision, page eighty nine."

Melinda gave in and thumbed through her accompanist hymnal to the correct page and belligerently pounded out an introduction, which flummoxed both Alice and the congregation. Harold Lasiter in the choir loft finally got the gist of where the song was going and jumped in, leading the rest of the choir in the way they should go.

At the end of the song Johnny Peters again took the podium, "It is time now for our offering."

At that announcement Adam Sloat stood and walked to the front of the church to pick up the two offering plates from behind the podium. They weren't where they belonged and he looked around a few seconds, then he spied them pushed all the way to the back, on top of the Bogen amplifier concealed in the podium. He nearly dropped the metal plates, when much to his surprise, the bottom plate was found to be quite warm. He handed the hot tray off to

Jake Neuman who had joined him up front to give a blessing for the offering, and to help pass the plates.

Jake yanked out his sweat soaked handkerchief and used it like a potholder before giving his quick prayer. "Lord bless the gift and the giver and let us always be thankful and generous. Amen"

Johnny finished his duties by asking for birthday offerings. "Do we have anyone with a birthday this week?"

LouElla Courtney squirmed at this question but didn't get up, so Amanda Adams helped her out. "Oh!" She squeaked, "It's LouElla's birthday this week. Isn't it Honey?"

Amanda knew full well it was LouElla's birthday. She also knew that LouElla didn't want anyone to know how old she was. "Did you forget your pennies LouElla?" She asked innocently. "Let me help you out!" Amanda grabbed up her purse and pulled out a little snap shut coin purse that just happened to be right on top and began counting out change. "Here's a nickel, and another and a quarter, well that's thirty five and oh, another quarter, that's sixty and one, two, thee, four, five, six, seven, eight, nine, oh let me open this other pocket. Oh my, I lost count. Where was I?" she asked.

The congregation answered, "sixty-nine"

"Oh thank you." Amanda smiled, "I just need six more pennies."

"Five" LouElla growled back.

"Oh!" Amanda squeaked again, "Honey have you forgot? You turn seventy five this year, same as my Uncle Ollie. You remember Ollie. He used to tell me how cute you were in school, and how he was your Beau for one whole school year."

188

Amanda's face had at first flushed red, but then with this final announcement had turned deathly white and for a moment Johny thought he was going to have to break up a fight right there in the choir loft.

Amanda held the change out to LouElla, who yanked it out of her hand, losing a penny in the process. Hubert pursued it across the hardwood podium until it came to rest beneath Malinda's feet.

Malinda let out a little yelp and turned aside clamping her knees together and pulling down her dress, as Hubert dove under the organ to retrieve the penny, knocking over the little fan and causing it to clang as it's blade banged against the metal guard. He held tightly to the penny, and after a couple of tries got the fan to stand up again, though it was aimed in the wrong direction.

"Here you are Miss LouElla" Hubert said as he handed her the penny. "Do you have enough now?" He asked innocently. "I have a little change if you need it."

LouElla looked daggers at Hubert and took the penny and marched down to the men holding the plates. She dropped the change in the plate Jake was holding and stood dutifully as the congregation recited. "Many happy returns of the day of your birth. May sunshine and gladness be given. And may our dear Father prepare you on earth for a beautiful birthday in heaven."

At the final word, LouElla sniffed loudly and turned and shuffled back to her seat in the choir loft.

"Let us spray." Adam Sloat mumbled and then went on, "Lord thank you for our blessings. Let us be generous like Ananass and Saphire was. Amen."

189

A few of the congregants looked a little doubtful at this prayer, but let it go.

Malinda had reached down and turned the fan back around the correct direction after Hubert had left, and was ready to go as Adam and Jake began to pass the plates. She started out her offertory with "When the Roll is Called up Yonder" but somewhere in the middle it turned into what seemed to be "Anchors Away" and then finished up with something no-one recognized except Marvin Trammel who used to play with a traveling country and western band. It may have been played on an organ and the timing butchered, but he would recognize Kitty Wells', "It Wasn't God Who Made Honky Tonk Angels" anywhere.

Adam and Jake finished up the last person on the last row before Melinda finished her offertory and she played blithely on, determined to use her allotted time. George Mason hurried to the back to gather up the plates and take them to the kitchen and lock them in the cabinet above the refrigerator. As church secretary, he did this religiously every Sunday, keeping the little key to the cabinet in a small box in the freezer of the refrigerator. It was a little hard to get the key out this Sunday since no one had defrosted the refrigerator for several weeks and the freezer door was sticking shut.

Malinda wound up her song with a few furbelows just as George returned and Johnny stood to speak again. "I am sorry to say our preacher for today," Johnny stopped and consulted his notes, "a Reverend J.L. Lincoln is not present, so church will be dismissssss.........."

"I am Jeremiah Lamentation Lincoln" A little, old, black man stood at the back entrance of the Fourth Street Baptist church, and at the sound of his voice, everyone turned and looked, the sound of the rustling of the padded pews the only thing to be heard.

"Uh. Uh." Johnny stood staring.

Melinda got up from the organ and joined her husband towing him toward their pew.

"Greetings to you in the name of our Lord from the Thirty Second Street Baptist Church in Kansas City Missouri." J.L. walked to the front as he spoke.

"I feel it is such a privilege to speak to you dear brothers and sisters in Christ." J.L. was in fact thrilled with the idea of bringing some good hellfire and damnation to Fourth Street Baptist church. "I must apologize for arriving so late, my assignment from the Southern Baptist Association was unclear as to the location of this church, and I had needs to find a phone booth on the way into town to search out the address. Then I found that the church had no phone, so I ventured into the large Baptist church down on Garrison and they sent me here."

He pulled out his handkerchief and put it down next to his Bible on the podium. He made sure the microphone was turned off, and walked to the side of the podium and spoke, "The world is full of tribulation. Do I hear an Amen? "

"I think we're 'sposed ta say somethin'." Tommy Worth spoke up.

"Shush!" Alice Worth looked around to see if anyone else had heard.

"That's right son! You are supposed to say somethin'. Give me an Amen!" J.L. grabbed the bull by the horns. "Amen!"

A few of the group mumbled "Amen" and J.L. had his first little victory.

"We are born to trouble and tribulation. We are born to struggle all our days. We are given life in pain and suffering and we spend our days in sorrow! Do I hear an amen!"

"Amen" It was a little louder this time as a few of the congregation got into the spirit.

"We are born into sin. Did not the Psalmist say, "Wash me throughly from mine iniquity, and cleanse me from my sin. For I acknowledge my transgressions: and my sin is ever before me. Against thee, thee only, have I sinned, and done this evil in thy sight: that thou mightest be justified when thou speakest, and be clear when thou judgest. Behold, I was shapen in iniquity; and in sin did my mother conceive me."

One "amen" came out of the crowd without prompting, and LouElla noted that it was that Edwards man that had moved here from out of town not less than ten or twelve years before.

"Amen?" J.L. asked.

"Amen!" the crowd rejoined.

"We cannot succeed upon our own. According to Romans thuhreeeeee.....Twenty thuhreeeeee...... For all have sinned, and come short of the glory of God!"

"Amen?"

This time the congregants "Amen." was a little more tenuous.

"We do many things in this world that are good. We give to charities, we help with food drives for the needy, we are courteous and kind." He hesitated here, "Well, we are courteous and kind when it is convenient." He paused here waiting for a little chuckle from the congregation, but only the sound was of Jake Neuman squirming in the unpadded pew, his back-side sticking to the polished oak.

"We are, however, generally good people." J.L. continued.

"Amen" the crowd liked the sound of this a little better and spoke up on their own.

"We come to church. We say our prayers. We sing in the choir and we send our hard earned cash to missionaries to save the heathens!" J. L. paused again.

"Amen" It was a fairly strong sound this time.

Then, J.L. let roar with all his power, "And we are all condemned to burn in hell for eternity!"

J.L. paused and Tommy took his cue while everyone else was silent. "Amen!" he shouted with enthusiasm.

"We have no hope of salvation in ourselves." J.L. spoke in a conspiratorial fashion. "We are weak and have no power to keep ourselves from burning in the everlasting lake of fire. We can not follow the law given to Moses without fail. We cannot get to heaven under our own power. We are lost."

Five minutes of the sermon was over and not one soul present was asleep. Even Hubert was wide awake. It was a first.

"You give your money, but God doesn't allow you to buy your way into heaven. You read your Bible, but God doesn't allow you to read your way into heaven. You could sing good Baptist hymns every Sunday morning for your entire life, but God does not let you sing your way into heaven."

"The road is wide and straight leading down into the fire. It is easy to walk upon and wide. In Luke sixteen nineteen we read," J.L. picked up his well worn bible and turned the pages and then spoke without actually looking down at the text, "There was a certain rich man, which was clothed in purple and fine linen, and fared sumptuously every day; And there was a certain beggar named Lazarus, which was laid at his gate, full of sores, And desiring to be fed with the crumbs which fell from the rich man's table: moreover the dogs came and licked his sores. And it came to pass, that the beggar died, and was carried by the angels into Abraham's bosom: the rich man also died, and was buried; And in hell he lifted up his eyes, being in torments, and seeth Abraham afar off, and Lazarus in his bosom. And he cried and said, Father Abraham, have mercy on me, and send Lazarus, that he may dip the tip of his finger in water, and cool my tongue; for I am tormented in this flame."

"The rich man found the value of Godliness too late. The fire burnt him and was not quenched and he suffered for eternity. He suffers yet as we speak!" J.L. bit off his words to emphasize each one.

"But my friends." It was time to bring them into the fold like sheep "The Lord God has a plan to keep us from that everlasting fire. God has perfectly conceived and executed that plan."

"Amen"

J.L. played the congregation masterfully. "God gave the greatest of all sacrifices to cover all our sins." He paused and received a few "Amen"s.

"We don't have to read God's word every day to get to heaven. But it is very, very good to read God's word and be spiritually fed. We don't have to sing praises all day every day, but Psalms one hundred, verse one, says "Make a joyful noise unto the Lord, all ye lands." We don't have to give until we are paupers, but God loves a cheerful giver." Jeremiah reiterated his earlier points quietly and then burst forth, his voice ringing through the building and reverberating out of the fellowship hall, "But God says we must pray to Him. We must believe in his son Jesus as the Son of the living God. We must ask forgiveness and we must repent! I say," Jeremiah continued after his voice cracked with fervor, "We must repent to avoid eternal damnation!"

Jeremiah didn't expect any "Amens" and was surprised to hear a few.

J.L. savored the dreadful silence and added forcefully once more. "Sinners, you must repent."

"Oh!" This time, Amanda Adams squealed like she had been stuck.

"I never." burst from LouElla Courtney when Amanda elbowed her again.

"Repent and throw yourself upon the mercy of the Lord. Repent you den of vipers and yield to God's calling and someday you will move on to a Heavenly reward. Amen! And again I say Amen!"

J.L. stepped down from the podium to the empty (unpadded) front row of the church, and spoke gently to the little group. "Repent, here and now. Repent where you stand or walk down here and I will join with you in prayer and make your repentance public as the Lord God has ask us to do. Repent, which is to say, turn your back on your evil ways and walk in the light and glory or our own Jesus Christ our savior." As he said this line he strode across the church and then quickly turned back to demonstrate, then bowed his head and spoke softly but firmly. "Lord I ask your forgiveness for my sins and ask Lord that you convict the hearts of those here in my presence to do likewise. I have sown your seed, and you will give the increase." At this point he raised his eyes and said, "Let us pray together as the Lord did teach us to pray, Our Father, which art in heaven, hallowed be thy Name. Thy Kingdom come. Thy will be done, in earth, as it is in heaven. Give us this day our daily bread, and forgive us our trespasses, as we forgive them that trespass against us. And lead us not into temptation, but deliver us from evil. For thine is the kingdom, and the power, and the glory, for ever. Amen."

As the sound of the congregation faded to silence Jeremiah continued. "If our talented organist will return to her instrument, we will sing a final song of invitation."

Melinda quickly stepped to the organ and kicked off her shoes and began to pedal, the bellows wheezing and the knuckles on the pedals clicking away as she built up enough pressure to play.

"I see from the program that page one-hundred and nineteen was the chosen song." Melinda was gratified that he was using that days program, "I could not ask for a better or more appropriate song for us to sing to show our devotion to our dear Lord and Savior, Jesus Christ."

Melinda began the introduction as Jeremiah motioned the crowd to stand. "A lady from England by the name of Charlotte Elliot wrote this song. She was an invalid, unable to go out and be part of society. She couldn't be part of a church, a family, like this one, even though her brother was the preacher to the local congregation. She could, however, be an influence throughout the world and throughout time, by writing these words. And he began to sing in a wonderfully modulated baritone voice, "Just as I am, without one plea, but that Thy blood was shed for me, and that Thou bid'st me come to Thee, Oh Lamb of God, I come! I come!"

As they sang through the verses, Jeremiah became silent, his head bowed, standing alone there in front of the congregation. Johnny forgot to walk back to the front as the song ended and was caught by surprise when the final "I come." was sung. He stepped out into the aisle and turned to the crowd and intoned his normal end of service lines, but this time, he really meant them, "Thank you Mr. Lincoln for your message and thank you, to all of you who attended. May God bless you and keep you until we meet again."

Mrs. Courtney was offended beyond belief to have this wrinkled little man accuse her of being a sinner. Why he practically called her a hypocrite right to her face. Miss Amanda just figured if the shoe fit, wear it and didn't help out Mrs. Courtney any. Mrs. Courtney stayed home for two weeks and then started checking before hand who was preaching, calling Melinda Peters to find out. If there was any question about the speaker, she just listened to the Old Country Church on her radio. She also cut back on her offering, but no-one noticed.

Tommy Worth, who was there with his grandparents, said it changed his life, or at least the results did. As an attentive thirteen year old he listened to every word and then announced on the way home from church "I might as well give up on salvation and just live as I wish. From what that preacher said I wouldn't never make it to heaven no-way."

Tommy's father whipped the notion out of him.

Amanda Adams invited Mrs. Courtney to club once. Mrs. Courtney had the Idea that club would be a group of women having snacks, drinking tea and doing good in a quiet sort of way, without spending any money or costing anything. This club was different.

Lucien Wainsford was the power behind the club. She owned the biggest car lot in town, and William Wainsford III, her son, ran it. William Wainsford the second, Lucien's dear departed husband, had started the dealership as a personal favor to Henry Ford to hear her tell about it. Lucien had plenty of money and plenty of pull, and was a pillar of "Club". It was a matter of pride to the ladies to find a destitute family and raise them up out of poverty and squalor both with their money and with the teaching of wisdom. Either the money or the wisdom must have been burdensome because most families declined to be a project after just a few months. New families to help were always in demand. Mrs. Courtney had no money for such foolishness. She had gotten that money the hard way. She had inherited it from her father. Club was not for her.

Club Charity

Lucien Wainsford and Sally Yates sat in the L&M Restaurant sipping cups of coffee and nibbling at fresh breakfast cake that Enos Mack baked every Thursday for the coffee crowd that rolled in around nine thirty in the morning.

"I tell you Lucy, them Slope kids is just sad, and the Mrs. Slope, why I swear she looks starved." Sally practically swooned about the "new" family she had found for club to help. "They are just what we are looking for."

"So where is Mr. Slope?" Lucien was yet to be convinced.

"Well now Lucy, he tries really hard. He's one of those fellers that jumps on and off a trash truck every day dumping cans of trash." Sally expounded on what she actually knew which was the man living at the Slope house was a trash hauler."He works every day out in the hot and the cold and the rain. Why, he has probably carried your trash out of your own back yard."

"And you say the wife is agreeable to some help from Club?" Lucien stumbled over her words as she took a sip of her coffee that Sarah the morning girl a the L&M had just "warmed up" for her. "Lordy, that's hot." She picked up the little metal cream pitcher, peeked inside and gave it a sniff, and then poured some into her cup, until her coffee turned a soft brown. "Well get me the address and Me and You and some of the other ladies will make us an appointment to visit with, what did you say her first name was?"

"She said it was Jessie, but I looked her up in the records at her kids grade school, you know I am good friends with Jane there in the office, and it said her name was Jezebel M. Slope. and the kids is named Samuel and Sharon." Jane there in the office, had neglected to tell Sally that the last name on the kids records was Raines.

Lucien had made up her mind. "Well tonight I will call the girls, and we will set up a time to visit with our new charity case."

The two days passed slowly until Saturday when several of the ladies would have an opportunity to join Lucien and go visit the "Slope" home. Several of the ladies had driven by the house down on Third Street and all agreed that the place looked promising. There were obviously kids there, indicated by the toys in the yard.

There was also a broken down Hupmobile with no wheels in the yard, and a dog living underneath it.

The meet and greet with the Slopes started off badly, with the dog from under the Hupmobile jumping on the driver's door of Lucien Wainford's brand new Ford (courtesy of Wainford Ford Inc.), wagging a cheerful greeting and slobbering on the window. A dirty faced child, wearing an adult's coat over a pair of nondescript britches, rushed to her car and grabbed the frayed rope on the dogs neck and pushed the dog back under the old car sitting in the front yard on blocks, and then joined him there.

"Was that Samuel or Sharon?" Lucien asked Sally.

"Well, I'm not sure, but the child did not have a dress on, so it must have been Samuel." Sally answered.

However, it was obvious as soon as Mrs. Slope came out on the porch that Sally's logic was faulty. A woman, very possibly a pregnant woman, came out the front door to stare at them, wearing the same outfit as the child, with a haircut that matched, looking like it had been done by the application of a large bowl and poorly sharpened scissors.

Lucien was taken aback by this apparition, but Sally had already gotten out of the car and was greeting the woman on the porch.

"Hello Jessie!" Sally squealed as she strode toward the porch. "I told you I would bring my friends from club."

Jessie stared at the women emerging from the cars with equanimity and said to Sally, "I hope they don't expect no tea or cocktails or sumpin cause I ain't got nuthin in the house and the water and electric done been turned off again cause that lout Slope ain't paid the bill for months. Even the beer's warm."

"Oh no Jessie. We don't expect anything from you. We came to talk to you about helping you out a bit." Sally came near hugging Jessie, but Jessie squirmed out of her reach, leaving Sally standing on the porch steps, with one arm extended stupidly. Just then Sally got a whiff of something from the porch and staggered back down the steps trying to escape from the smell. It seemed to come from the house. Sally suddenly realized her arm was still extended and she dropped it down to her side feeling foolish.

"Mrs. Slope? My name is Lucien Wainsford. You may call me Mrs. Wainsford or Miss Lucy if you wish." Lucien stepped forward boldly to get a better look at their new project.

"Why the hell would I call you anything?" Jessie asked, looking down at Lucien standing at the bottom of the steps.

Lucien, not sure she had heard correctly continued with her spiel, "We are the Carthage Women's Charity Club or CWCC and we understand you talked to Sally about some bit of help we could offer you."

Jessie stared at Lucien as intently as she would have had Lucien been at the freak show and had two heads. "What the hell are you talking about? And stop calling me Mrs. Slope. I ain't married to that bastard."

Just then three of the other ladies had joined Sally and they all stood there with their mouths hanging open.

"Well ain't that a sight Sharon?" Jessie said to the child under the car. "These here women catching' flies with theys mouths hanging ajar is gonna charity us. Ain't that sumpthin?" She then turned back to Lucien who was too stunned to move, "My name is Jezebel Raines and that no-good Joey Raines is the only husband I ever had and he done moved out, and so me and Slope was sposed to be splittin' the rent and the 'lectric and such, only I ain't got a penny to my name 'causin that lousy Joey ain't paid no alley money or child sport 'causin he says we is still married cause them papers ain't gone through no judge yet."

Judy Fletcher had walked up to the porch during this diatribe holding a grocery bag with various items in it, chosen with care by the group as a first bit of help for this poor women. Judy was holding the bag in her arms and gaping at Jessie. "We brought….uh….we….."

"What did you brung woman?" Jessie swiveled her attention from Lucien to Judy, "Spit it out! What did you brung?"

Judy, losing her nerve entirely, shoved the bag into Sally's arms and retreated, her heals snapping on the limestone sidewalk as she hurried back to her car.

"Lordy, what's the matter with her?" Jessie asked as she watched Judy practically run away. "Did I scare that poor child?" Jessie laughed as she took the sack from Sally's arms. "Sharon and Sammy! Come outen there and see what these nice ladies done brung us!" At that Jessie started to poor the contents of the bag out on the porch. "Well hell! This here is soap and shampoo and crap. What are we 'sposed to do with that? We ain't got any water you know!" She said loudly as she continued to dig through the products now poured on the dirty porch floor.

Two children with identical haircuts and almost identical outfits crawled out from under the car, one of them towing the dog by the frayed rope around it's neck. The other end of the rope now seemed to be tied around the child's wrist "What you got for us Momma?" The child leading the dog asked.

"Why Sammy these kind ladies brought us fancy smelling soap." Jessie tossed one of the little fish shaped pieces of soap to the child and the dog, thinking it might be a treat grabbed the soap in mid-flight and swallowed it down.

"Pete! Pete! Don't eat no soap Pete!" the child holding the dog rope began to bawl. "Momma, make him throw up like you did Sharon when she drank the antifreeze."

This statement made all the club ladies jump, but they held their ground watching the little drama.

"A little soap won't hurt no dog Sammy." Jessie squatted down next to the boy. "Pete eats all sorts of stuff that would make you barf your socks up and it just slides right down." Jessie petted Pete and he gave Jessie an affectionate lick on the ear. "Maybe it'll make his breath better! Lord dog! Your breath still smells like that roadkill squirrel you been chewin' on."

While this scene was playing out, two of the other ladies had gone back to the car where Judy was studiously picking at her fingernails, and brought a couple of boxes. These boxes contained government commodities. The ladies carried the boxes to the porch and sat them down and then retreated back to the car to join Judy.

"Oh!" Jessie shouted as they sat down the boxes. "It's that peanut butter like your Daddy's brother done give you!" The two children ran to see, drawing the cans out of the box and staring at them. Pete joined in, sniffing and slavering over the sealed containers, apparently able to tell that they contained things better to eat than soap.

"We done got some of this here government food from that lousy bum daddy of therin Joey Raines. His brother lives out to Colorado and so we went out to visit and by God weren't we surprised to get to Dooranger Colorado to find his brother was livin' on the Ute Indian reservation with some red-skin woman that was twice his age. They gived us boxes of this here crap and it was a good thing, cause all the food we took had gone bad in the truck on the way across Kansas, well excepting the beer, and we was hungry as bears. If Joey hadn't come across a 'bandoned car with gas he could siphon off, why we wouldn't even o' made it to Dooranger. Joey was always lucky that way, findin' stuff he needed right when he needed it."

Lucien had stood quietly through this entire scene. Sally on the other hand, had let out little sounds, squeaks and chokes as Jessie expounded on Joey's good fortune. Finding her voice, Sally finally put in a few words. "Well if these things will help then we will try to get you signed up for the program so you can have your commodities delivered to you. We just have a few papers to fill out."

"Now I don't know about no commodities coming to my house. I ain't no beggar." Jessie stared at the food, "And besides, Slope brings us perfectly good food from the truck stop. If we didn't get it, it would get thrown out to the hogs. We does OK on that."

That made both Sally and Lucien jump.

"I'll have to think on whether I want them green govment cans around the house where folks would see 'em." Jessie went on. "I don't want my friends to see I'm one of them leeches, what lives ofn their neighbors." At that, she leaned down, tore off a part of the box lid, sorted a bit and chose one of the rectangular cans that said, "potted meat products" on the label. She pulled the tab and poured the lump of meat out onto the cardboard flap she had torn off. She handed it to the child not attached to the dog, and said, "Share this with your brother and don't feed too much to Pete." Jessie turned back to Sally and said, "I don't know why they don't just put "Spam" on the can, cause eve'body and the dog knows that's what it is."

The little girl grabbed the lump of meat and took a big bite out of it, before handing it to her brother. "Mmmmmm" she said and licked her filthy fingers after her brother took the meat for his turn.

Lucien stared at this and her stomach began to roll. "I think we best be going." She said to no-one in particular and turned to leave.

Sally still stood her ground, "We need you to fill out some forms Mrs. Slo…. uhhh I'm sorry what did you say your name was?"

"Raines. I am, for now, Mrs. Joseph Raines, married to a no-good thieven' Ute indian." For the first time Jessie looked sad. "Well, maybe he ain't a Ute, but his brother is."

Sharon, who had finished off her portion of the meat and was sorting through the cans a bit more, held one of the cans in her hand and tugged at her Momma's shirt. "Momma, this has Pete's name on it! They done brought something for Petey." The girls dirty face was filled with wonder as she stared at the can.

Jessie reached down solemnly and took the can, "Oh girl, it says pe......" and Jessie paused, "Why baby it does say Pete on it. We'll share it with him in a bit OK?" Jessie held the can out to Sally to show her where it said "Pet Milk" on it and winked. "I reckon these ladies knowed we had us a fine pup that needed some milk."

The last Christmas before DeWalt retired was loud at his house. However, it had been uneventful, with no phone calls from the station. He had eaten turkey, watched football as the Green Bay Packers lost, and played with the grandkids toys until nearly six in the evening. A nagging feeling like something was missing had been hanging about. Like that feeling you have when you've just gotten seated at a wedding and your wife leans over as the ceremony starts and says "Did you unplug the iron after you ironed your shirt.?"

DeWalt wasn't sure what this nagging feeling was until Ernie, the oldest grandson, asked if Grandpa wasn't going to that crazy ladies house, like always. Then DeWalt knew what had been bothering him. So DeWalt decided to go check on Mrs. Courtney. He told his wife where he was going and she assumed he had gotten a call, and she had just missed the phone ringing amidst all the mayhem, but he set her straight. He bundled up, climbed in his car, and headed down to Mrs. Courtney's. It was just a few blocks but he was thoroughly cold by the time he arrived. The heater in the car had just started having some effect when he reached her house. It looked deserted when he pulled up. No lights shone through the windows and the front curtains were standing open, an unheard of event after dark. He went to the front door and to his surprise there was a note taped to the door. With the light from the hospital parking lot across the street, he could just make out that it had his name on it. He walked back out to his car, slid in the front seat and turned on the dome light. He opened the note and read, "DeWalt, I knew you would come check on me. You know where my key is. Come in and turn on the coffee." DeWalt left the marginal warmth of his car, got the key from under the flower pot and entered Mrs. Courtney's house. He went back to the kitchen, and *there was a percolator on the stove ready to turn on. There was another note on the table. "DeWalt, Your pie is in the refrigerator wrapped in plastic wrap. If you haven't already, turn on your coffee, go ahead and do so now. Your cup is right there with the sugar, a spoon and a fork. I am not home today. My niece called. I have gone to have Christmas with her and the children. I have never done this before. I know you like a quiet time on holidays, so have your coffee, and pie. Don't wash the dishes. I'm sure you would chip the pot or break the percolator. Don't forget to turn off the stove and the lights. I can't afford those awful gas and electric bills now. LouElla Courtney."*

DeWalt had his pie and coffee, soaked up the silence for a few minutes, and then went home.

When his wife asked "How was LouElla?"

He said, "She's fine. Just fine."

The End

Other Books by Allen Dean

CyberCrime

A "two books in one", mystery/thriller

comprised of

Life & Death

A role playing computer game gone awry.

and

The Real World

Where the game spills over into reality.